WATERSHED

WATERSHED

ELIZABETH HARLAN

Viking Kestrel

With special thanks to Josh Harlan for his generous sharing of editorial
and technical skills throughout the preparation of this manuscript

VIKING KESTREL
Viking Penguin Inc., 40 West 23rd Street, New York, New York 10010, U.S.A.
Penguin Books Ltd, Harmondsworth, Middlesex, England
Penguin Books Australia Ltd, Ringwood, Victoria, Australia
Penguin Books Canada Limited, 2801 John Street,
Markham, Ontario, Canada L3R 1B4
Penguin Books (N.Z.) Ltd, 182–190 Wairau Road, Auckland 10, New Zealand

First published in 1986 by Viking Penguin Inc.
Published simultaneously in Canada
Printed in USA by The Book Press, Brattleboro, Vermont
Set in Times Roman
1 2 3 4 5 90 89 88 87 86

Library of Congress Cataloging in Publication Data
Harlan, Elizabeth.   Watershed.
Summary: Two teenage brothers, Jeb and Noel, face a great many difficulties
in the aftermath of a disastrous prank which sends one of them to jail.
[1. Family problems—Fiction.   2. Brothers—Fiction.
3. Conduct of life—Fiction]
I. Title.
PZ7.H2262Wat   1986   [Fic]   85-40835   ISBN 0-670-80824-5

For my sons Josh and Noah,
who brighten my days and
lighten my life

AUTHOR'S NOTE

In July of 1981, during one of the hottest, driest summers ever recorded in New Jersey, four Pequannock Township young men were arrested and subsequently convicted for entering a blockhouse and, according to *The New York Times*, "turning on a pipeline valve that led to the collapse of a section of an aqueduct supplying sixty percent of Newark's water. . . . All four were charged with malicious damage, a felony punishable by up to ten years in prison."

Although my novel is entirely fictional, *Watershed* was inspired by the tragic implications and consequences of such a real-life event.

WATERSHED

1

"Hey, Jeb, what would you say the high point of your life has been? You know, the absolute best thing that ever happened to you?"

We were lying on the grass at Doc Coulter's place this afternoon, taking a break after mowing the back of the property, when my brother Noel asked me that. Beyond the stream I could see a farm tractor in the distance. It looked like a Matchbox John Deere weaving back and forth across the fields.

It felt like Noel's question came from the clear blue sky. I can still see the way he tossed his hair from his eyes and gave me that I-dare-you look of his. Noel's hair is straight and blond like the color wheat turns in the fall. Mine is brown and wavy and impossible to make look any other way than wild. I was lying on my stomach pulling clumps of crabgrass out of the earth, but when Noel asked that, I got up on my knees and answered without even thinking.

"Easy! This past spring when I took first in the three thousand meters at the All Eastern."

What I didn't say was what happened later, when my girlfriend Stevie and I drove up to the reservoir and spent until midnight on a blanket under the stars. But that's none of Noel's business. He'd probably've said something super macho about getting laid. And Stevie and I haven't gone that far yet. Anyway, it's our business what we do and don't do, and nobody else's. For the last few weeks nothing at all's been going on, because Stevie's been away visiting her grandparents in Florida.

Since I wasn't supposed to be driving after dark yet, Dad almost took my driving privileges away for good that night, but he finally settled for a week. I think he was plenty proud of how I did at the meet.

Then I asked Noel for the high point of his life. He told me it was the day he was born, which was Christmas. That's why his name is Noel.

"How can you say the day you were born is the high point of your life?" I asked him. "No one can even remember that."

"Because ever since then my life's gone downhill," he said.

I didn't know what to say, so I just kept yanking clods of weeds from the earth and wishing Noel hadn't said what he did. I had this strange feeling that what was happening to me right that moment was recording itself in my mind, that I would always remember it and everything that surrounded it—the arid countryside, the parched farmland, the unending heat—long after the moment was over and gone.

Then, breaking up my stream of thought, Noel laughed his dry, sarcastic-sounding laugh and added, "I guess I did a pretty good job of spoiling everyone's Christmas that year. I mean with Mom having to go to the hospital on Christmas Eve and all, and then her being away for Christmas, it couldn't have been too nice a time for you and Dad."

"What do you mean, spoiling my day?" I asked him. "It was probably the last perfect Christmas I had. After that I had to have *you* around all the time, and that's when things started to get bad!"

Noel landed a punch on my arm and began laughing, which lightened things up again.

Since nothing much was going on this summer, Noel and I put together a lawn-mowing business. But the weather's been so hot and dry, it seems like the grass has just given up growing. Most of our customers put us on an every-other-week schedule, which means we're only taking in half the money we were counting on.

The way we work our lawn jobs is by alternating. One place I ride and Noel pushes, and then we switch for the next place, because riding's much easier and lots more fun. The system works out well enough, except for the Coulters' place on Morningview Road.

They've got almost three acres of lawn and enough trees to make a forest, so whoever pushes really has to kill himself trimming around all those trees. And Coulter counts every blade of grass you miss so he can tell you all about it the next time.

We use a Kabota riding mower and an old push model for trimming. It's our family's equipment, but Dad lets Noel and me use it for our lawn business on the condition that we pay for maintaining it out of our earnings.

When we first struck the deal with Dad, Noel didn't think it was fair that we had to pay all the maintenance expenses, since Dad would have to pay practically as much by himself if we weren't using the equipment. But when he brought that point up, all Dad said was, "Well, if you want to start your own business, you'd better learn what it takes to run it."

Noel started to give Dad some lip, but I told him to lay off or he'd completely blow our chances of getting the mowers. Noel and Dad never see eye to eye on anything anyway. And they never have, as far as I can remember.

Noel's sixteen, a year younger than I am and a year behind me in school. He'll be a junior in the fall. He's not much of a student, and I guess you'd have to say he has some problems getting along with people. He's always had a chip on his shoulder, maybe because a lot of things that've come easy to me, like getting good grades and being good at sports and stuff like that, have never come easy to him. At school he's pretty much of a troublemaker, and at home he fights with Mom and Dad over practically everything: haircuts, studying, the music he plays, the food he eats, you name it.

The funny thing is, as different as we are, and I guess we're pretty different in a lot of ways, Noel and I have always been close and gotten along well.

When we were younger, it felt as though the two of us practically owned the world. Our world was the woods and the farms all around Wakefield, where we live. There was always something to do, and Noel and I were always busy out there doing it.

When we were little we used to love to hide in the cornstalks on the farms around our house. We'd play this game where we'd lie in ambush for the enemy, and then when we got bored with that we'd run wild up and down the rows, which are kind of like alleyways, until we'd lose track of where we started.

If the farmers had ever caught us in there stomping around in their corn they'd have crucified us, so it added lots of thrills to lie low whenever we heard footsteps or voices or a car slowing down on the road nearby. We'd watch each other turn red in the face holding our breath till the threat of someone coming was gone. Half the time I think we faked hearing something just to make it more exciting.

Mom always says that when Noel was little he had an awful time trying to keep up with me. I was fifteen months older and did lots of things like walking and talking early. Noel must've begun life with the feeling of being in a never-ending race with someone who's been given a winning handicap.

Still, there were some things Noel could do that I could never have done if it weren't for him. He was always lots bolder and braver than I was, and when it came to trying something new and scary, he would always be the leader. There I'd be stuck in the mud and scared to take a step, and Noel would already be way out in front, right in the

7

thick of whatever it was he wanted to try, calling back to me to come along.

I remember when we were just little kids—maybe eight and nine or something like that. For a couple of summers around that time our family used to rent a house down on the Jersey shore. Our younger brother, Pete, was just a little baby then, and Mom had to spend a lot of time in the house with him.

When Mom wasn't on the beach, Noel and I were supposed to stay out of the water and just play in the sand, but of course we always wanted to be in swimming. At first we'd stand on the shore looking out kind of wistfully, then before you knew it we'd be jumping the little low breakers, and soon we'd be all the way in.

Noel had a kind of fearless streak. I'd always be amazed at how he didn't seem at all scared when I'd be completely freaked out. One day I remember asking him how he could dive right through one gigantic wave and not be afraid of the next one that was coming. "You can't let yourself be scared," he told me. "If you're scared, the waves know it and they come and get you. Only the scaredy-cats get dragged under."

Maybe the idea of being a scaredy-cat got to me, but something made me want to prove how brave I could be. All of a sudden I went running out into the ocean, diving through one wave after the other, trying to *feel* like I wasn't scared.

The waves weren't all that bad, but the undertow was something fierce. I got caught in a swirl of water somewhere down below, and before I knew what hit me I was being tossed around like a piece of driftwood. I began to swallow whole mouthfuls of water, and I panicked and began screaming for help. Noel actually got out to me in time and saved me. Little as he was, the guy managed to get an arm around me and started swimming for the shore. The whole time he was pulling me in he was gasping, "You're OK, Jeb, you're OK. Just don't let them know you're scared."

We never told anyone about that, because we weren't supposed to be swimming in the first place. But I've never forgotten how brave Noel was, and to this day I'm absolutely certain that I would've drowned if it hadn't been for him.

Something must've gone really wrong for Noel somewhere along the line, though, because now that he's big his life just hasn't been so great. Somehow all the things he seemed so good at when he was younger don't count anymore, and the things that seem to matter as you get older, like school and sports and girls, don't seem to work out for him.

The two of us always used to go running together when we were younger, for example, but ever since Noel tried out for varsity track last year and didn't make it, he absolutely never runs anymore. Just gave it up cold, which is really too bad, because the coach told him—and I know it's true because he told me too—that in another year Noel would almost certainly make the team. *If* he kept working. But the problem with Noel is he doesn't seem to want to work at things like that. Or maybe he just can't stand the feeling of defeat. And I guess if there's one thing

I know from my own track and cross-country experience, you sure have to learn how to lose if you ever want to have the chance of winning.

When I was seven and Noel was six, Pete came along, and he's always been treated like the baby in the family, with Mom running interference for him in family fights and Dad being lots softer on him than he ever was on Noel or me.

Pete's a completely different kind of kid from us. Even the way he plays is different. It's nothing like the games Noel and I played when we were his age. Pete's real quiet and inconspicuous, and most of the time he's off in his own little world. Mom always says I'm the "stable, responsible son," Noel's her "wild Indian," and when it comes to Pete, she just says something like, "He's no bother at all."

One of Pete's favorite activities is taking himself down to the dump to find some piece of junk. He brings it home and paints it or puts it together with some other "treasure" he's collected on another scavenging mission, and then he comes up with some wild story about the meaning of his new invention.

A couple of years ago Pete found this old stovepipe and painted it gold and connected it to the top of a rusted metal garbage can. He told anyone who asked that it was an ancient shrine from a vanished tribe of Indians who once inhabited the region. He even invented a name for the imaginary tribe: the Slopokum Indians. I'm sure he got the idea from "Slowpoke," which everyone in our family calls him because he moves so slowly all the time.

Pete'll tell you how these Indians were very gentle and

calm and always took lots of time with the peaceful kinds of things they did, instead of whooping it up and racing out to make war the way other tribes did. You just know when you hear him describing the Slopokums that he's talking about himself.

Pete's even got this imaginary Slopokum friend, an invisible boy he calls Maypo. Supposedly Maypo got caught in a time warp and landed up in our local garbage dump here in New Jersey. Pete believes Maypo's always with him wherever he goes. He even sets a place at the table for Maypo, unless company's around, and then he gets embarrassed.

Once in a while I come up to Pete when he doesn't know I'm there, and I can actually hear him talking very quietly, explaining in this patient, teacherly way about whatever he's doing, and I can tell he's imagining that Maypo's with him.

The other thing about Pete is how sensitive he is: almost to the point of being hypersensitive. Maybe because Noel's closer in age to him, or maybe just because Noel's a pretty unusual person too, he seems to understand Pete better than anyone else in our family. Noel acts very protective about Pete whenever the little guy gets worked up about something.

A couple of weeks ago, for example, our cat Charlie had a litter of kittens in a low cabinet where Mom keeps some pots and pans. When we found Charlie in there in the morning with her four little kittens, Mom made a place for them in the mudroom. Even though she laid down Charlie's favorite mat and put her food and water bowl nearby, Charlie obviously didn't go for the idea of having her family moved, so one by one she picked up her kittens in her mouth and carried them back to the cabinet. Mom took them out a second time and then shut the cabinet real tight so Charlie couldn't get back in.

Sure enough, Charlie started to meow and scratch at the door. When Pete saw her doing that he got real upset and started to scream that the kittens would die if they couldn't get back in their home, and how cruel Mom was being. While Mom was busy trying to explain things to Pete, Noel went over to the cabinet and started pulling out all the stuff in there. When Mom asked him what he was doing, Noel told her that if pots and pans were more important to her than real live animals, she must be a pretty awful human being.

The whole scene ended in a big fight between Mom and Noel, and Pete still blames Mom for having "abused" Charlie, which is really pretty funny coming from a little kid talking about a spoiled house cat, but Mom doesn't find much humor in it at all.

Getting back to Noel and what I was saying before, the strange thing is, I remember it differently from the way Mom tells it. I mean, I never was particularly aware of being ahead of Noel. In fact, it always felt like there was a whole way in which he was ahead of me. From the time we were really little, Noel seemed to know absolutely everything there was to know about nature and the outdoors. He knew lots about animals—what they ate, where they hid, how you could find them—and lots about bugs. He's always been crazy about insects, any kind of insects, but especially cicadas, which he knows as much about as anyone, I imagine.

For years now Noel's kept this huge cicada collection. Pete acts as his junior assistant, and as the collection gets bigger and bigger, the two of them build more and more specimen cases. The basement's become practically wall-to-wall bug cases.

It's true that I've always been the one to get good grades in school, but that's something anyone can do. All you have to do is listen in class and read what you're told to. Even Noel could do it if he wanted to, but he just doesn't. He's into something else, something entirely different from what school's all about.

I guess Noel's a country kid at heart, but even though we live in a farm community with animals and crops all around us, we're not really a farm kind of family. Dad's a lawyer and works in New York. Still, Noel's always been more farm-oriented than the rest of us. He even used to say that he wanted to be a farmer someday. I don't think Dad was real impressed with that idea, though, because I remember his telling Noel, "It's a tough way to make a living, farming is. You can't rely on weather very well."

Noel looked real hurt when Dad said that, and then he shot back with, "Not like the way you can rely on people to break the law."

Dad told him not to be so fresh, and I think that was the last time Noel talked about being a farmer.

2

Yesterday after we finished work, Noel and I were sitting on the lawn in front of the house, trying to figure out something to do which would either end before dark, since I can only drive during daylight hours, or which we wouldn't need a car for, so we could get home whenever we wanted.

All of a sudden we looked up and saw Pete coming down the street with our dog Hank alongside of him. There was blood running down Pete's face and onto his shirt, and you could hear him crying from all the way down the block.

We ran over to him to see what happened, and when we got there Noel tore his shirt off and wiped Pete's face, which was pretty scratched up. After Pete settled down enough to talk, he told us how he got hurt. It seems he was playing this game he likes with Hank. The idea for this game started a while ago after one of Pete's missions down at the dump, where he found a leather harness-type thing that's made for Seeing Eye dogs. The leather was torn in parts, but Pete put some lengths of clothesline together to fill it out and fitted it onto Hank. Then he started pretending he was blind and letting Hank lead him all around the neighborhood.

"It was all this guy's fault who tried to run us over," Pete was saying between sobs. "This guy in a car comes by and tries purposely to hit Hank and me, so Hank had to push me over into a tree in order to save my life."

"Hold on a minute, Pete," I told him. "What's this about a guy in a car purposely trying to kill you?"

"He *was* trying to kill us, or Hank would've never pushed me into the tree." Pete leaned down and patted Hank.

"Don't you think maybe it's not such a great idea to play this game of yours out on the road?" I asked him. "I mean, you could get yourself really hurt one of these days."

"It's not a game. I'm training Hank to be a Seeing Eye dog so he can save blind people's lives," Pete said.

"Sounds more like it may be working the other way around," I told him, but he just leaned down and grabbed Hank's collar again and started walking off toward the house with his eyes closed, his hands patting the air in front of him like a blind person would do. When he was just about at the house, he turned around and called back to Noel, "By the way, I saw one of those cicada bug shells on the tree I bumped into. It was in perfect shape. You'd've loved it, Noel."

"Whoa, come back here," Noel called to him. "Come show me where, hey? Would you, Pete?"

"Yeah, I'll show you if you want. Come on." And suddenly Pete was all happy again and running back where he just came from, only now he wasn't acting like a blind man anymore, that's for sure.

Noel and I followed him to the tree down at the corner of Overlook and Elm. It happens to be an elm tree, a big huge one with an immense trunk. I bet they named the street for this very tree.

Pete leaned real close and started inspecting the bark, and sure enough, there, stuck on like it might come loose any second, was this brownish plastic-looking case, about the size of my thumb or maybe even smaller.

"Wow, this blind man sure can see!" Noel said, as he leaned in real close to examine the shell. "The cicada probably just emerged. Otherwise the molt would've already fallen off and been destroyed. It's much too delicate to last like this for very long."

"Where do you think the cicada is now?" Pete wanted to know.

"It could be anywhere, near or far," Noel told him. "Sometimes if you're patient and just wait awhile, you get lucky and find it somewhere real close by."

"Let's be patient and wait awhile," Pete said.

"OK by me," Noel said, and sat himself right down on the ground under the tree with his legs stretched out in front of him.

Pete and I sat down too. We sat there quietly, just

waiting, not even saying anything for the longest time. It was hot and humid, and it felt good in the shade.

Noel had his feet stuck out almost in my lap, and I was staring at the hiking boots he had on. He wears them all the time, summer and winter, and sometimes Mom teases him about sleeping in them too. They're real old and worn out and have these little leather sprockets attached to the tops of them, which go up to his ankles. The laces—one is brown leather like the boots and the other is red—are tied together in lots of little knots, and in a couple of places the laces missed the loops. You could tell Noel must not have been looking when he laced them. It doesn't matter to him just as long as the boots hold together on his feet.

"Listen," Noel said after a while. "You can hear them, lots of them."

It was true. Once he said that, we could hear them all around. You couldn't see them, but you could hear the strange kind of singing sound cicadas make, like a high hiss.

It was really neat the way we finally saw one. All of a sudden Noel jumped up and said, "Follow me, and keep as quiet as you can." Then he led us to a little mound of earth a few feet from the tree, pushed aside some leaves and twigs, and there it was: an incredibly perfect specimen of a cicada.

The thing was large enough and close enough to see each segment where it joined the next. You could actually almost *feel* the smoothness of the veiny-looking forewing. And its eyes, its bulging beady red eyes, had a shining non-wet look to them. It's hard to describe.

The cicada stood there absolutely still, almost like it knew it was being watched. It was awesome. We watched for a real long time. At least it felt like a long time. I couldn't even say if it was seconds or minutes or more. It felt like the whole entire living world had converged in this tiny insect. And then after a while, the cicada didn't seem tiny anymore. It seemed like it got suddenly magnified into some gigantic creature. As though we were tiny and it was enormous. It was weird.

Then the cicada broke the trance by hopping out of sight. And I felt myself breathe, really breathe, for the first time since I saw it. I realized I must've been holding my breath.

"Hey, where'd it go?" Pete was the first to speak.

"I don't know. Away, I guess," Noel told him. "Maybe it didn't like the company."

"Can we find it again?" Pete asked him.

"Maybe not that very one, Petey, but you'll find lots of others this summer. This is the summer when the seventeen-year cicada is due to emerge in the north here," Noel said. "We hear them all the time now, so that must mean they're coming out."

"How come they all know it's time to come out?" Pete asked.

"Nature, I guess," Noel said. "How come baby birds know when it's time to fly from the nest?"

"But why do they call them the seventeen-year cicada?" I asked Noel.

"That's how long it takes for them to mature. When cicada babies hatch—they're called 'nymphs'—they bury themselves underground. Then when these nymphs are fully developed, which takes seventeen years, they dig their way up through the ground and come out into the world."

Pete said, "It's a little like growing up and leaving home," which when you think of it is really a pretty smart thing for a ten-year-old kid to say.

"Righto," Noel told him, and you could tell he thought Pete was pretty clever too.

Suddenly a cicada—maybe the one we'd been watching—flew up right in front of us, and a big black flying insect came out of nowhere and attacked it, right there in midair, not even fifteen feet away.

It looked like the black flying thing was traveling a hundred miles an hour, too fast to tell what kind of insect it was, and when it reached the cicada, it made a zinging, crackling sound, a little like the sound one of those backyard bug zappers makes when it traps a bug.

"Wow," Noel said, "catch that! It's a cicada killer. I've never seen one do that!"

Noel sounded more excited than I've ever heard him sound. He just kept saying "wow" over and over again, as we watched the cicada killer trap the cicada in its wing and carry it off across the sky.

"What *is* a cicada killer?" I asked Noel.

"It's a wasp," he said, "a killer wasp that only goes after cicadas, which is why they gave it its name."

"Does it eat the cicada, Noel?" Pete asked. "Is that why it kills it?"

"The wasp doesn't actually even kill the cicada when it attacks," Noel explained. "It only poisons the cicada with its sting, which completely paralyzes it. Then the wasp

19

carries the paralyzed cicada off to bury alive beneath the ground in a cell. Once its cell is 'provisioned'—that's like getting groceries for the house—the mother wasp lays her egg right on the immobilized body of her victim. Then she closes up the cell and leaves the cicada there to live like that for several weeks. When the wasp egg hatches, the larva, or baby wasp, feeds off the cicada."

"Gross," Pete said when Noel finished describing all this.

"Not really," Noel told him. "It's the law of the jungle. You know, survival of the fittest and all that."

"So," I asked Noel, "the only purpose cicadas serve in nature is to feed the killer wasp larvae?"

"I suppose," Noel said. "That and to fill the forest with song in the summer, when thousands of them are born, or born again, depending on how you think about their life cycle."

"Strange," I said. "It hardly seems worth all the trouble of being born and grown, to wind up ending your life that way."

"It's not exactly like cicadas get to make choices, Jebbo," Noel said.

"Yeah, I guess you're right. Human life is different," I said.

"*Some* human lives are different. The lucky ones," Noel corrected me. "Most of nature has no choice in how it lives and dies. No say in the matter."

"Hey, can I take the cicada's shell, Noel?" Pete asked. "For our collection?"

"You mean the molt. Yeah, sure," Noel told him. "Bring

it down to the basement and we'll save it with the cicada specimens."

By the time Noel and Pete took the cicada shell to the basement, it had gotten too late to make plans for the rest of the afternoon. Before we knew it, Mom called us all for dinner.

And then after dinner the phone rang. I heard Dad pick it up and say, "Yes, Mr. Robinson. What's this about your hayfield? . . . My son Noel?"

The next thing I knew, Dad stomped into Noel's room and started yelling at him. I couldn't hear what he was saying, but when Dad came out of Noel's room a few minutes later, I heard him tell Mom, "That boy's not leaving the house for the rest of the evening."

3

The next day was one of those sweltering August-in-New-Jersey days when the heat and humidity just beat every ounce of energy out of you. At around three o'clock Noel and I decided to take a break, even though we'd only mowed half the lawns on our list.

We left the equipment on the Stevenses' lawn at the corner of Elm and Prospect and wandered up to Cow Hill. You get an incredible view of the whole Wakefield valley from up on top there: all the big squares and rectangles of farms, each with its own type of crop growing. It looks from a distance like some kind of carefully plotted geometric gridwork.

When we got to the top of Cow Hill, we popped open

a couple of cans of Coke from the six-pack we had along with us. Everywhere you looked you could see the hot parched countryside just wilting away from lack of rain. This summer's drought is supposedly the worst in the region for as long as anyone remembers. They say it's been so hot and dry that the potatoes are actually cooking in the ground.

From where we were sitting up on Cow Hill, we could see old man Robinson disking his lower field beyond the treeline, where the potatoes had just been harvested. Today was hot but clear, and we could easily make out his big yellow tractor moving slowly across the field. A whole bunch of seagulls were flying in his wake, diving for earthworms that get turned up with the soil.

"Hey, what was all that with Amos Robinson's call to Dad last night?" I asked Noel. "I heard him giving you hell when he got off the phone."

"Oh, you know. One of those typical scenes where Dad was overreacting as usual. I'd been taking a walk through Robinson's field—the one over by the stream—and I had Hank along. He must've caught the scent of a rabbit or something and tore into a couple of piles of hay. That was all. Then Robinson called to complain and Dad barged into my room and started screaming so loud I'm sure everyone in the neighborhood heard every word."

"What'd you tell Dad?" I asked Noel.

"I told him to cool down, that all we did was accidentally mess up some hay waiting to be baled in one of Robinson's fields. But it was obviously the wrong thing to say, because Dad got even angrier."

"What'd he say?" I asked.

"You should have heard him. He was in full legal gear. 'What do you mean, *accidentally* messing up someone else's property? How can something like that happen *accidentally* when you weren't supposed to be trespassing in those fields in the first place?' "

"It sounds like Dad, all right," I told Noel.

"Don't you just hate it when he uses legal words like *trespassing* for ordinary simple things like taking a walk? I told him we weren't trespassing, and then he wanted to know what my *intention* was when I was in Robinson's field. I thought the veins in his neck were going to pop when he said the word *intention*."

I laughed and told Noel I knew what he meant. I was beginning to get a real clear picture of the scene.

"When I told him I didn't have any *intention*, that I was just taking a walk with Hank, that's when the shit really hit the fan. Dad started shrieking at the top of his lungs. 'That's *all*? When are you going to learn that trespassing on private property is illegal and that whether it's a person or his dog that damages another man's property, the person is the one who's held legally responsible?' "

"Maybe you shouldn't've pushed him so hard," I told Noel.

"Well, I did try to lighten things up, but you know Dad has absolutely no sense of humor at times like that. I asked him if he thought they could send Hank to jail."

"Oh, come on, Noel, you didn't!"

"The hell I didn't. You know what Dad said then? 'They can't send a dog to jail, but they sure can send that mutt to the pound if you don't keep him on a leash.' "

"You were asking for that, Noel."

"Yeah, well, I let it go. No use wasting energy on a lost cause. Dad's hopeless when it comes to reasoning with him, so mostly I don't even bother trying anymore. And of course he got the last word. He always does. Just as he's leaving my room, he turns around and marches back in like some sort of tragic hero and delivers one of his soliloquies on spoiled kids."

Noel dropped his voice about two octaves and went on.

" 'You don't know when you've got a good thing going. Nobody but yourself to be responsible for. You get everything you could possibly ask for, and then what happens? Instead of finding something constructive to do, you go out and find some trouble to get into.' And then he stomps out and slams my door."

Noel laughed the whole thing off like it really didn't matter, but I know my brother well enough to know that things like this really get to him. It's not like he's so sure of himself that he needs to be put down by Dad all the time.

I guess what I wish is that Dad could be more tolerant of Noel and just accept him a little more for himself rather than always trying to make him over into some kind of person he's just not meant to be.

Sometimes I try to imagine what my father must've been like as a kid growing up. There's a picture of him in his high school yearbook when he was a senior. It shows this real straight type of kid with very short hair parted all the way over on one side of his head.

In the yearbook they have these captions underneath the pictures of all the graduating seniors, and the one for my father says, "Charles Gray, Class President: He wishes not to seem but to be the best." It can be a hard act to follow, having a father like that.

We were still sitting up on Cow Hill drinking Coke and looking out over the farm fields when Noel said, "That guy Robinson's really bad. Do you know he actually filches water from the town by dredging over into the stream to fill his irrigation ponds?"

"How can he do that without getting caught?" I asked him.

"Easy. Farmers are always dredging their ponds. How's anyone gonna prove that a little low land between the town's water and a farmer's pond didn't happen by natural causes?"

"But doesn't anyone ever catch him while he's doing it?" I wanted to know.

"Sure, people've probably seen him do it," Noel said. "But who's got the nerve to blow the whistle on Robinson? He's the biggest potato farmer in Easton County—seven hundred and fifty acres of French fry futures."

"Jeez, no wonder Robinson's got so many irrigation lines going," I said. "It looks like an airborne Niagara Falls over his farm. Most of the farmers have stopped irrigating because they don't have any water left in their ponds."

"That's right. They'll all lose their crops, just you watch, while old Potato Head makes out like a bandit. And all us guys are told not to wash cars or water lawns or shower so much so we can save water."

He squeezed his empty Coke can with one hand and then grabbed another one from the pack, shook it up real hard, and popped open the top, so the Coke shot straight up in a big fizzy geyser like water shooting out of an irrigation pump.

"Someone oughta really teach that bastard a lesson," Noel said.

I figured Noel was still reacting to Robinson's call to Dad and that was why he was so angry about "old Potato Head," but I knew it wouldn't do much good to bring that up, so all I said was, "What kind of lesson did you have in mind, algebra or geometry?"

"Very funny, Jebby," Noel said in a sarcastic tone of voice.

He's about the only person left who ever calls me Jebby anymore, and the only time he does it is when he's teasing me.

"Actually, I've got an idea," Noel said. "What if someone threatened Robinson's water supply, so it looked like maybe *his* potatoes might have to go without water and cook in the ground?"

"Yeah, but you just said he filches water for his irrigation pond from town water, so how could his water supply run out as long as the town still has reserves?" I asked him.

"Well, if the town reserves ran dry, where would Robinson filch his water from?" Noel looked like a five-hundred-watt bulb lighting up. "You know that block-house that controls the pipelines from the reservoir, the one that sits back there in the woods above Robinson's house? It has a sign on it: NO TRESPASSING. PROPERTY OF THE NORTHPORT WATERSHED."

"Yeah, I know what you mean," I said. He and I must've spent hundreds of hours of our lives hiking around in those woods near the blockhouse he was talking about.

"What if someone got into the blockhouse and turned on the valve that controls the water supply from the reservoir? Wouldn't that be a gas?"

"Not if the water from the reservoir was wasted, it wouldn't be a gas," I told Noel. "Then we'd all be without water, not just Robinson."

"Yes, but Robinson's house is right below the reservoir, only a few thousand feet away. So he could be the first to find out. It would just be a scare, Jeb, not a real disaster or anything. When the water started pumping, someone could call in the emergency to Robinson, because he lives right there. He'd have a fit and report it right away. It'd never get to the point where the reservoir ran dry. Not once Robinson heard about it. He'd go stop up the pipeline with his thumb if he had to."

Noel was laughing real loud and wild now, and even though I could see some humor in this grand plan of his, the whole thing sounded pretty far out.

"I don't know, Noel. It sounds like a lot of kicks, but it's also risky."

"No risk, kiddo, no kicks," Noel said, and I could tell he was already getting his mind set on pulling this plan off. And when Noel makes his mind up about something, all of Hell's Angels couldn't change it if they tried.

After mowing the rest of the lawns on our list, Noel and I walked over to Robinson's farm to watch his horses grazing. You could tell they were really hungry for the new growth of nice fresh green grass on the other side of the fence. They'd obviously been eating down their own grass as fast as it was growing up, so now they were sticking their heads through the split-rail fence to get at the high grass on the other side.

"I bet Amos Robinson's too cheap to give his horses grain once the grass gets going," Noel said, still sounding angry from before.

"They sure do look hungry," I said. "Look at the chestnut mare over there. She looks like a giraffe, she's got her head stuck out so far."

"Hey, I've got an idea," Noel said. "Let's let the poor horses have a little picnic on all that nice high grass. We'll just take out a couple of rails back here where no one will notice."

"I don't know, Noel," I told him. "Robinson's already on the warpath. I don't think we need to give him more reason to be angry."

"He'll never know we did it. We'll make it look like an accident, like the horses just dislodged some rails at one of the posts while they were eating."

I was going to raise another objection, but something made me hesitate. I guess I was feeling a little like a party pooper. I mean, I had just put down the idea about opening up a valve at the blockhouse, and now here I was putting down this other idea which, when you got right down to it, seemed pretty harmless. I thought back to myself as the ten-year-old boy standing on the shore protesting, while my bolder braver younger brother was charging ahead fearlessly into the surf. I suddenly felt like this time I didn't want to be left behind.

One of the rails was rotten, and as we were lifting an end out, it broke in two. We decided just to leave the two pieces of broken rail lying on the ground. Then we got out of there real fast, before anyone saw us.

When I came down to breakfast this morning, Noel shoved a copy of the Saturday edition of the *Wakefield Weekly* at me. The front-page story was staring me in the face:

Apparently a herd of hungry horses at the Robinson farm on Morningview Road pushed through their pasture fence to graze on the surrounding fields. It seems the old adage has been proven true once again, that *the grass is always greener on the other side.*

There was a huge photo taking up practically the whole bottom half of the front page which showed about a dozen horses grazing on the lawns of the nearby development, Brooktree Estates. There were all these mothers standing outside their houses watching their kids bringing carrots or sugar or something over to feed the horses.

The article went on to tell how the police were finally called—they sent a whole bunch of squad cars—and how the cops used laundry lines and kids' jump ropes to lasso the horses and lead them away.

When I looked up from the paper and over to Noel, he practically spit out a mouthful of orange juice, he was trying so hard not to laugh out loud. Then Dad, who was sitting across the table from Noel, said, "Robinson's damned lucky nothing more serious came of this."

"Like what could've happened?" Noel asked Dad. "Other than someone's flowers getting nibbled a little bit." You could hear that fighting edge in Noel's voice, the way he sounds whenever he and Dad are going at it.

"If one of those horses had gotten up to the road," Dad

said in his most serious-sounding voice, "it could've caused a serious accident with a passing car. It's been known to happen. If someone got killed or even hurt, Robinson would have hell to pay in liability. A suit like that could cost a man a million dollars!"

"Boy, Dad, you really look on the bright side of things, don't you?" Noel said.

"I look on the realistic side of things," Dad told him. "And I don't appreciate your snide attitude, Noel."

After that, I couldn't get it out of my head that someone actually might've gotten hurt or even killed from what we did. I hadn't thought about that possibility before. It kind of took away the simplicity of the whole thing, put a damper on the fun. Suddenly I was feeling this nervous kind of fear inside, that something awful could've happened.

I guess we were lucky this time. And lots of other times when we've done stuff like that. And the way I feel now—with senior year coming and college after that and a whole bunch of other things—maybe I don't feel like pushing my luck too hard anymore.

4

A week's gone by since Noel cooked up this idea
to raid the blockhouse. It seems like he hardly thinks of
anything else anymore, as though suddenly this whole
thing has become some sort of obsessional revenge plot
to get back at Robinson. It's almost like Noel blames
Robinson lately for everything that's gone wrong in his—
Noel's—life, which of course is absurd, because Robinson's just this crotchety old farmer.

It's the beginning of the Labor Day weekend, and this
afternoon, Friday, Noel and I were trying to figure out
what to do with our last really free weekend before school
starts up again. Suddenly Noel pulls out this map he drew
up of the countryside around the reservoir.

Without any explanation or introduction or anything, he starts tracing possible access routes to the blockhouse with his fingers. Lying there on his stomach plotting out his course, he looked just like a big overgrown kid with one of those board games we used to play when we were young. Then all of a sudden, Noel sits up real straight and says to me, totally serious, "We don't want to approach the blockhouse from the town, or afterward someone might remember seeing us going back in that direction."

I got a really freaked-out feeling when Noel said that. I guess it drove it home to me that this thing is real, at least in *his* mind, and not just some dumb kid's game.

Take the map, for example. When Noel pulled it out, I couldn't believe how good a map he'd actually made. To really appreciate how into this thing he is, you have to understand that even though he's plenty smart, Noel barely passes his subjects in school because he never does the work. But this map is unbelievable. Definitely good for an "A" in any class he might've done it for.

The wooded areas are shown in fuzzy swirls of green. He probably used Pete's crayons to do it. And there are patches and strips of carefully shaded blue where all the ponds and streams are located. And then Noel must've used a darker, smoother blue, like a marker pen would make, to show the reservoir. It draws your eyes right to it, there in the middle of the map, like a magnet.

And the place names—the streets and roads, the town line, even the name of Cattletrail Bridge—they're all printed out real tiny and neat in black ink. Noel must've spent hours working on it.

So while he's lying there, kind of casually tracing routes

with his fingers, Noel suddenly announces, "Monday's when we do it, Jeb. Labor Day is it. What a way to end the summer. Whoopee!"

I didn't say anything, but I must've looked a little surprised, because Noel went on to explain.

"Monday's it, Jeb. If we wait any longer, the dry spell will end. A huge storm's due after the weekend, sometime next week, and then the whole point'll be lost. No one's going to give a damn about a little wasted water after that. And anyway, we don't want to do this thing once school starts. We won't have enough time if we wait."

"I don't know, Noel. This is pretty serious stuff you're talking about doing."

I didn't know what to say. I guess I felt cornered and was stalling.

"Chicken out if you want to," Noel said. "I'm going ahead. I'll just know you can't be counted on."

"Hey," I reminded him, "I never agreed to this in the first place."

"Look, Jeb, I don't need you or your approval to do what I want to do, so just go ahead and cop out if you like."

It really made me mad when Noel said that, but it was all happening too fast for me to know how to react, so all I said was, "Don't give me this crap about copping out, Noel."

He seemed to get the message finally, and this time he didn't make some snide remark. After saying nothing for a couple of seconds, all he did finally say was, "Sorry, Jeb. I was just counting on you."

That got to me when he said he'd been counting on me, so I said, "I'll think about it. I have to give it some more thought."

"Jeez, Jeb, some things aren't a matter of *thinking*. Sometimes you just have to go ahead and act."

"And sometimes acting without thinking can get a guy into a mess of trouble," I told him.

"You sound just like Dad," Noel shot back at me in this really snotty voice. "Let me know by the end of the weekend, by Sunday, Jeb." And then he repeated, "Because Monday's it. That's when we go." Then, real fast, to change the subject before I said anything else, Noel asked if I wanted to see the new Spielberg movie at Cinema II.

"Sounds good," I said. "I'll see if I can get the car this afternoon in time for the four o'clock show. Stevie's due back from Florida today, and we made plans to get together tonight."

When I went inside and asked Mom for the car, she told me she needed some groceries for dinner, which kind of threw my timing off. I asked her if I could get them after the movie let out, but she said, "Not if I want to make dinner before dinnertime comes, Jeb."

"Noel and I will just make ourselves a sandwich or something when we get in," I said.

"You're not the only people who need dinner tonight."

"You know Dad," Noel piped up. "The old meat-and-potatoes king would never settle for sandwiches for dinner."

"Noel, I really don't like your attitude sometimes,"

Mom told him, but I grabbed him by the arm and started dragging him toward the door before he could make things worse.

"We're leaving now, Mom. I've got the list," I called over my shoulder as we went out the door.

I could tell the moment I turned onto Olden Road that I should've gone the other way, through Ridley, but I figured that was probably a mess too. I had to downshift in all the traffic, and I ground the gears a little as I did it. I guess I was pretty impatient, since it was already past two o'clock.

Noel put his head back the minute we hit the traffic— he can't stand being stuck in traffic, never could—and looked like he was dozing off for a while. Noel's the kind of person who can fall asleep anywhere and anytime. He can even do it in a room full of people. Sometimes I think he does it kind of as a way of escaping. When the pressure's on, or he doesn't like the scene, he just kind of fades out of the picture.

It seems like this summer every bridge in every direction everywhere you go is down for repairs, including the bridge down Mill Road to Cottoncreek Junction, which really messes things up for practically everyone who lives in the area.

There are about a dozen different stories about how the bridge broke in the first place. They all have something to do with an oversized truck that shouldn't have been there.

The real question is, when are they going to fix the damn thing? Apparently Easton and Flint counties share responsibility, since one ends where the other begins, which just so happens to be in the middle of the stream that the bridge crosses over.

A car screeched to a halt behind me as I slowed up behind a line of backed-up cars at the intersection of Olden and Stevens. Noel woke up with a start, looked around for a moment to get his bearings, and then started right in with complaints about the traffic.

"Just what I've been thinking," I told him, "while you've been catching forty winks. It's all because of the Mill Road bridge being out. Hey, do you have any idea of how many months Easton and Flint have been wasting time arguing over who has to pay for the repairs?"

"It seems like years already," Noel said. "You know, when you think of it, adults are always complaining about how kids are so irresponsible and how we argue and fight with them over every little thing, and how we have to get our way, et cetera, et cetera. But when you really look at the facts, adults act more like children than kids do."

5

By the time Noel and I got in line at the checkout counter at the Super Fresh, it was nearly three o'clock. Noel was all fidgety about the time, because he didn't want to be late for the movie. It would take at least half an hour to get home, then another few minutes to unload the groceries, and then we'd probably hit more traffic when we headed over to Cinema II. So it looked pretty close in terms of time.

The woman in front of us had a cart full of groceries and a little kid wriggling around in the seat in back. While we were waiting in line, I checked Mom's list.

"What do you think Mom wants, Noel, ground round

or ground sirloin? She just wrote down hamburger meat on the list."

"How should I know which one she wants, and anyway what difference does it make?"

"Twenty cents a pound is the difference it makes," I told him. "Maybe you should take this back and get the ground round instead."

I handed Noel the package of ground sirloin that I'd taken from the meat counter, but after looking at the label, he tossed it back down into the shopping cart and said in this embarrassingly loud voice so the lady in front of us overhears and even turns around, "Jeez, Jeb, you're talking about a lousy half a dollar. You'd think we were poverty-stricken the way you're carrying on about a couple of cents a pound."

"Keep your voice down, you're embarrassing me," I told him, and decided to keep the sirloin. It didn't seem worth the hassle to go through exchanging it. And besides, I kind of agreed with Noel's point about the difference not being worth worrying about, even though I was annoyed about the scene he was making.

I checked the last items on Mom's list. A gallon of milk and a dozen brown eggs. Mom always says she likes brown eggs because they remind her of the ones she collected as a little girl from the hens on her grandmother's farm. When I try to imagine Mom as a little girl, I always picture her looking just like Fern on the cover of my old copy of *Charlotte's Web*. Mom read that book to me when I was little, and I guess I kind of got her and Fern mixed up in my mind. When Mom was a girl, she actually had short curly blond hair, like she does now, and Fern's hair is brownish and longer, more like Stevie's.

"This is taking forever," Noel grumbled. He grabbed a pack of M&M's off the rack next to the checkout counter, tore them open, and poured the whole pack into his mouth.

The checkout lady looked up, horrified. "Hey, kid, you haven't paid for that yet."

"That's because you haven't given us a chance to pay for anything for the last half an hour," Noel shot back.

"Now just hold on here," the checkout lady said.

She got real red in the face, and the woman with the kid in front of us was looking back and forth between Noel and the checkout lady like she was at a tennis game. The kid in the shopping cart started bawling its head off suddenly and then wriggling all around and practically falling out of the cart. The mother had been trying to write a check to pay for her groceries when the thing with Noel and the M&M's started, and now she was trying to pick the baby up and write the check at the same time.

I really thought she was about to drop the kid, so I just blurted out, "Here, let me hold the baby while you do that."

I don't know where I got the nerve to do that, but I just wanted to get out of there as fast as I could.

The mother turned around with the crying baby dangling from her arms and passed it to me, saying, "Would you really hold him for a moment?"

"Sure thing," I said and took the kid from her.

It was a little like being thrown a pass in a football game and not being ready to receive it. I kind of grabbed hold of this screaming kid and automatically started doing these things I've seen mothers do when they hold their babies, things I must've seen Mom do when Pete was real little. I patted its back a little, and the most incredible thing happened. The baby actually stopped crying. It kind of pulled back and away from me a little bit and just looked right at my face. Then it smiled this big smile with just one tooth in its mouth and practically poked my eye out with its finger.

The mother and the checkout lady were suddenly acting real nice and amazed about what a fantastic way I have with babies, and I have to admit it felt kind of neat. I didn't really know what to say, though, so I just smiled back at the kid.

Then the mother took her baby back and thanked me. As she wheeled her cart away, she told this whole long line of women at the next checkout line, "I hope my little Christopher grows up to be such a nice young man!"

It made me feel really good.

As we were leaving the supermarket, Noel says to me, "I would've liked to shove that pack of M&M's down that dumb checkout woman's throat. How'd you like the way she acted like I was some kind of thief? Like I'd really steal a pack of candy and then eat it right in front of everyone!"

"I can see her point of view, Noel. I mean, lots of people just help themselves to little stuff like candy and never pay for it."

"And thanks to you and that little angel act you put on, we're way too late to catch the movie now."

"Hey, hold on," I told Noel. "Being late has nothing

to do with my holding that kid. I only did it so we could get out of there quicker."

"Well, by the time we get home and dump this junk, it'll be at least four," Noel said, "and we'll never make it to the movies before four thirty. We may as well skip it. I don't feel like missing half the movie."

"Half an hour's not half the movie, Noel. Come on, let's go. There's nothing better to do."

"Nah, not me. I don't go to movies if I have to miss the beginning." Noel sounded certain, so I knew he wouldn't change his mind no matter what I said.

As long as we weren't rushing anymore, I decided to take it easy on the drive home. No sense killing myself in all the traffic when I wasn't going to get where I was going any faster that way. And besides, it was kind of nice just cruising along. I love driving with the windows down and the wind breezing through the car. It makes a nice kind of fast rushing noise.

Noel wasn't sleeping on the way home, but he was huddled over on his side of the car feeling angry and uncommunicative the way he gets when things don't go his way.

As I was driving I was thinking about that baby, Christopher. And then I started thinking about Stevie. I was wishing she'd been there to see me with the baby, and I was sort of rehearsing in my head the way I'm going to tell her about it the next time we get together.

Then I started imagining how Stevie is when I'm near her: her pretty brown hair that smells like soap and this rolled-up red scarf she wears around her forehead. I began to miss her a lot, like she'd been away forever and not just for a few weeks.

The way I met Stevie was through running. Last fall, when I was a junior, Stevie was the only freshman girl who made the cross-country team. From the first day I saw her, I had this tremendous crush on her. I'd see her out running in the afternoons, but we never really met or anything. And then I did the most embarrassing thing. I can barely bring myself to *think* about it anymore, let alone tell anyone about it.

I was thumbing through the local telephone directory, and when I came to the F's something clicked and I decided to look Stevie up—her last name's Farr—and see where she lived. I found out that she lives over on Havemeyer Drive, so I copied down her street address, which I didn't recognize but figured I could find, and got on my bike and rode over there.

It was a school-day afternoon sometime in the early fall. It had to be in September or October, because it was five or six o'clock and there was still plenty of daylight left.

When I got to the general neighborhood, I asked an old lady who was walking a dog where Havemeyer was, which was how I found Stevie's house. But what's really amazing is how much nerve it took to ask this little old lady who didn't know me from Adam which street Havemeyer was. I mean, she couldn't have had the faintest idea of who I wanted to find over there, yet I remember thinking the whole time that she'd probably know exactly who I was looking for and that somehow my being there would get back to Stevie.

I remember how hard my heart was beating when I got to the corner of her block. I was absolutely certain I'd run into her on my bike and she'd know for certain it was because of her that I was riding down her street.

Of course when I got there, all there was to see was a big white house with red shutters and a red front door. The mailbox in front said number eleven, which was the street address in the phone book. But I rode by so fast—I must've been going fifty miles per hour on my bike—that there was no way anyone inside that house could have seen who I was, even if it just so happened they were looking out a window at the right time.

A couple of months later there was a cross-country meet at East Bradley, and I was running with the boys' team. Later that same day the girls' team was out practicing the course for their meet the following weekend, and Stevie sprained her ankle on the trail. John Clugston and I were jogging along behind her when it happened, and that's really when we met for the first time. John and I helped her get up and then ran for first-aid help.

The first time I asked her out—it wasn't exactly like asking a girl out on a date—I went up to her after sign-up for spring track last year and asked if she'd like to run with me over the weekend. I think I said something like, "How about if I come by Saturday morning and we do ten K's along Cedar Brook together?"

I remember feeling good that it came out sounding casual. And I'll never forget the way Stevie looked when she answered. She smiled this enormous smile and opened her eyes so wide that she looked like a little girl who'd been given a big surprise. And then she said, real simple and direct, "Oh, I'd love that."

Girls are usually so cagey and cool. Most of them go in for the playing-hard-to-get routine. But Stevie's not that way at all. She just acts like how she feels. I think that's why it's easy to be so casual and natural with her. It feels really good to be able to be that way with someone.

Of course she never knew how come I found her place so easily, and I sure wasn't going to tell her about my biking expedition to check her house out before I knew her. She'd think I was some kind of lunatic. Actually, maybe she wouldn't. Maybe someday if we really get serious—engaged or something—I'll get up the nerve to tell her.

I was thinking all this stuff and feeling pretty good by the time Noel and I got home. I didn't even mind that we weren't going to see the movie. The thought of spending a nice relaxing couple of hours at home in the air-conditioned house, waiting for Stevie to call when she got home, was beginning to appeal to me.

I dropped the car keys on the counter and told Mom I wouldn't be needing them after all. That was when Noel came out with another snide remark about my making us late.

"If it hadn't been for Jeb playing up to some old ladies, we might've made the four o'clock show," he said and stomped out of the kitchen and upstairs to his room. I heard the door slam so hard I felt the whole house rattle.

"What's eating your brother, Jeb?" Mom asked.

"I don't know exactly. Lately he has this attitude that everyone is out to get him. Whatever goes wrong, it's someone else's fault for letting him down."

"You seem to understand him better than anyone else," Mom said to me. "Maybe you could try to find out what's at the bottom of it."

"I wish I could, but it's getting harder and harder. It's kind of like he's got this permanent grudge against everyone, and no matter what, he's just not going to give it up."

"Do you think Noel feels a little jealous of your relationship with Stevie? I mean, he knows she'll be back soon and you'll be spending less time with him."

"I think he feels that way a little bit," I told Mom, "but there's more to it than just that. Dad's always on his back lately about every little thing. No matter what Noel does, Dad's always criticizing him."

"I think Dad cares a great deal about Noel," Mom said. "But Noel makes it hard for Dad to reach him, and I guess sometimes your father's way of caring is to be critical."

"Well, maybe Dad ought to think about what *he's* doing wrong sometimes too."

Mom didn't say anything. She just kept busy taking groceries out of bags and putting things away. When she got to the last bag, a big smile broke out on her face, and she looked over at me like she knew just what was up.

"Bananas? Banana pudding? Pie crust? Ice cream?" With each item she pulled out of the bag her voice got a little louder. "Why, Jeb, I never use these ingredients. They weren't on my list. Whatever did you get them for?"

"Pizza, Mom. I thought I'd whip up a homemade pizza later. Couldn't you tell?"

Mom laughed, of course. I knew she would. I threw in those extra things because I was hoping she'd take the hint and make my absolute favorite dessert, banana cream pie. Mom usually makes it in the summer when it's hot.

Sometimes when I go shopping, like today, I pick up

all the ingredients and just bring them home with the other groceries. It may take a day or so, but eventually Mom'll come up with her banana cream pie.

"Well, I'd better go get showered before dinner," I told her. "Want me to stick that ice cream in the freezer before I go upstairs, or were you thinking of using it just now?"

"You go get showered, Jeb. I'll manage the rest of this stuff by myself," she answered, and I could tell by the way she was smiling that there was at least a fifty-fifty chance we'd be having banana cream pie for dessert.

I heard the front door open, and I knew Dad was home from work. As I headed upstairs, I was thinking how Mom has a very different kind of personality from Dad. Very laid back and relaxed and real accepting about the way people are. I think it has a lot to do with the fact that Mom's a weaver. Or maybe it's the other way around: her being a weaver comes from her being the way she is. Weaving's very different from being a lawyer like Dad. It's totally nonjudgmental, if you know what I mean. And I guess it makes her a lot easier to get along with.

I remember when I was a little kid coming home from school, if Mom didn't come out to the kitchen when I got home, I'd know she was working in her weaving room.

Mom never leaves her loom when she's into her work. Not for phone calls, not for meals, not for anyone or anything. And then if it's not what she wants, she tears out all the strands and starts all over again, until she gets it right. I once told her that I couldn't imagine having the patience to go through all that just to weave one small piece, and she told me, "But can you imagine the fun of being able to undo all your mistakes and start fresh again?" I always think of that when things don't work out for me the way I'd like them to.

It always amazes me how with all the mess in the weaving room—the newspapers and magazines, the piles of clothes that need sewing, the unfolded, unsorted laundry—Mom can sit there peacefully weaving away at some perfectly neat pattern. I know it drives Dad crazy. Lots of times he complains about how messy the house is, but Mom just comes up with some quote from one of the women writers she's always reading about how boring and uncreative housework is. She'd much rather weave than clean, and her favorite thing to say on the subject is, "Dust just returns to dust, so why bother moving it around?"

Sometimes when I was younger, Mom would explain the way the loom worked. She'd show me how to warp and explain what the weft was and what you had to do to make all those hundreds of strands of wool come together in a piece of cloth.

When I was twelve or thirteen, I made up a jingle about Mom's weaving. It had a line in it about Mom "rockin' and a-rollin'/ warpin' and a-weftin'/ yippin' and a-yelpin'," and I used to sing it to her sometimes when she wove.

It always made Mom smile, and if her weaving was going well, she'd start swinging her head from side to side in sync with the pumping movements of her arms and legs. When the weaving wasn't going so well, she'd get real impatient and tell me, "Shush, Jeb, I'm losing it. Go away."

Even when I was a little boy, Mom says I understood how important her work was and how happy it made her. One time for a Mother's Day present I made her a stick figure drawing of a woman weaving. The loom in the picture was an enormous boxy thing, but the weaver was even bigger, way out of scale. And on the face, which was a big wobbly circle, there was a long, turned-up line for a smile.

Mom still has that drawing. She framed it and hung it in her weaving room, next to all the frames of tied-up wool and little sample pieces of weaving.

6

I took a cool shower and felt all refreshed when I got out, but when I came out of the bathroom I bumped into Noel, who was standing there with his shirt off, waiting for his turn in the shower, muttering something about the air-conditioning breaking down.

"Damn house feels like a furnace already," he was saying. "And the air-conditioning just went off while you were in the shower."

"What do you think happened?" I asked him.

"I don't know, but when Mom called the service they told her they couldn't get out here until tomorrow, at the earliest. Everyone else's air-conditioning is breaking down too, I guess."

The heat's been so bad these past few weeks that the air-conditioner's been running nonstop. Apparently, it just decided to give up. Already, with it off for only a little while, I could tell the difference in the house, which was beginning to get a flat, humid feeling.

By the time I got down to the dinner table, the front of my red shirt, the one that says *Adidas* in black letters across the pocket, was already wet. Noel came down without a shirt and Dad looked up from the mail and told him to go put a shirt on for dinner.

"Nice way to say hello, don't you think?" Noel said as he left the room, and Mom, who was stirring something on the stove, said in her smoothing-over voice, "Charles, you *could* say hello to him before you tell him what he's doing wrong."

Dad didn't respond, just looked up from the mail he was reading. "Damn Public Service bills. I hate the way they do this, Laura. Call them in the morning and tell them we won't pay on any more estimated billings. If they can't monitor the usage monthly, they have no business charging for it!"

Mom didn't say anything, just went calmly over to her list of things to do that she keeps tacked on the wall by the refrigerator, and made a neat little note to call Public Service. All of a sudden it became clear to me how big a difference there is between the way Mom deals with Dad's demands and the way Noel does. I mean, it's obvious that the way Mom gets around feeling angry when Dad does something like he just did is by not letting it get to her. Noel would never let a thing like that go by without making a federal case out of it. I guess in a way I take after

Mom in this type of thing, which maybe explains why I get along better with Dad than Noel does.

When Noel came down, Pete was already at the table. He had an empty chair next to him with a place set for Maypo with plastic summer dishes that we usually only use outside. The rest of the table was set with the regular china plates. Pete says that since Maypo is an Indian from an ancient tribe, he's not used to the kind of breakable things that modern people use.

When everyone was sitting down at the table, Mom asked Dad how his day went, which is how dinner usually gets started in our house.

"I heard from Frank Coopersmith over at the court-house that that kid from Long Hill Road—what's his name, you know, the one who's always hanging out downtown with nothing to do but look for trouble—"

"Jesse Kawalski," Noel said. "Is he the one you mean?"

"That's right, the Kawalski kid. I could've predicted that one would land in jail when he turned eighteen. You could tell that boy was headed for trouble from before he cut molars. First it was stealing pennies. Then it was slashing bike tires. Next thing you know he was stealing cars. Well, this time he went a little too far."

"What'd he do?" Pete had a whole mouthful of potatoes when he asked that, and his eyes were open real wide like he couldn't wait for some really big story.

"Kawalski stole a register full of cash from Wright's Pharmacy and landed up with six months in jail. I congratulated Coopersmith when I saw him as I was leaving the courthouse."

"Is Coopersmith the owner of the pharmacy?" Pete asked.

Dad laughed. "He's the family court judge who heard the case, son."

"Was it a first conviction, Charles?" Mom asked.

"That good-for-nothing's been cooling his feet in juvenile court for years, getting away with murder while everyone's been giving him chance after chance to straighten himself out." Dad was really getting worked up now.

"Did he really kill someone, Dad?" Pete asked.

"The way he tells it," Noel piped up, "you sure get that impression."

"Your father doesn't really mean he murdered anyone, Pete. That's just an expression," Mom said.

Then Noel got back in the act with one of his snide remarks that never fail to get a rise out of Dad. "I thought lawyers were supposed to be real precise about the words they use."

"That will do, Noel," Mom told him.

"It's high time that troublemaker served some time." Dad was still on Kawalski's case.

"I suppose you don't consider Culver Juvenile Detention Center serving time?"

Noel sounded real belligerent when he asked Dad that, but Dad didn't get a chance to answer because Mom said, "You know, Charles, Jesse Kawalski's mother has had to hold down two jobs since her husband was laid off from the glass factory, and I'm sure it's taken a terrible toll on those poor kids to have her gone so much."

It's just like Mom to find a way of explaining why a

person could still be good and yet do bad things.

"Jesse Kawalski's no kid, Laura. He turned eighteen last month and should pay just like anyone else for what he's done wrong."

You knew from the way my father spoke that he meant to end the conversation. And then, to make sure that the subject got changed, he picked up his empty water glass, asked me if I'd get him some more, turned to little Pete, and asked him how his day had gone.

By now Pete was make-believe shoveling food onto Maypo's plate from one of the serving dishes, and when some of the potato and peas accidentally fell on the table, Mom suggested that perhaps Maypo could help himself in the future. Pete looked hurt.

"Maypo's not used to the way we give the food out here," he told her. "Slopokums do it different from us."

"I hope they do a lot of things different from us," Noel said in an angry-sounding voice, "because I think there's plenty wrong with the way people think and act around here."

Dad looked furious and told Noel that if he couldn't be civil he could just as well leave the table, which of course was what Noel wanted to do anyway. He grabbed his plate and went over to the sink, where he just dumped it, leftovers and all, and stomped out of the room and upstairs.

The rest of the meal was pretty tense and gloomy, with Mom trying to patch things over and Dad looking like he was having a hard time keeping hold of his temper. You knew he wanted to lay it on Noel in the worst way, but Noel wasn't there to scream at and Dad can't stand scenes at the dinner table, so he usually just sits there and fumes silently.

For dessert Mom brought out—guess what?—a banana cream pie, which was really kind of sad because no one was much in the mood for having any. I did my best to finish up my helping, and then when I was leaving the room to go upstairs, I went over and gave Mom a kiss and said, "Thanks for making the pie, Mom."

"Sure, Jeb, any time," she said, but I could tell from her voice, and from the wet, distant look in her eyes, that she was still feeling kind of down about the dinner-table scene with Noel.

When I got upstairs, I saw Noel had left his door open a crack, and when I peeked in I saw him lying there on his bed staring up at the ceiling, so I knocked and walked on in.

"Indigestion got you?" I asked him, trying to lighten things up a little.

"You know why he can't stand Jesse Kawalski? I mean the *real* reason he's got it in for him?" Noel was looking up at the ceiling.

"What do you mean, the real reason? You don't think it's enough that the kid gets into trouble all the time?"

"That's just the *excuse* for hating him. The real reason is that Dad can't stand anyone lower class. It's all that rot he's always handing out about kids who come from 'the wrong side of the tracks.' "

I knew what Noel was sore about. He was thinking of times when Dad gets critical of some of the kids *he* hangs around with, the ones like Ben Bullock and Roger Koestler who get into trouble around school and town all the time.

"I can't stand it when Dad gets on his high horse about 'backgrounds,' " Noel was saying. "He just loves that expression about how the apples don't fall far from the tree. In fact, Dad loves all sorts of stupid, simpleminded catchy phrases. I think it's easier for him to deal with mindless generalizations than actually to think about things."

"Aren't you being just a bit hard on him?" I said. "I mean, Jesse Kawalski's no angel, when you think of it. And he was what started all this tonight, wasn't he?"

"It's not just Jesse Kawalski, Jeb. That's the thing you don't seem to get. It's anyone, everyone who comes from a 'bad background.' " Noel made the sign of quotation marks with two fingers on each hand. "Dad's got a thing about practically anyone who's not rich and successful the way he is. He's always talking about making 'good contacts' "—he made the quotation mark sign again—"if you want to succeed in life. He thinks corruption and evil and bad character and things like that are like germs lurking everywhere in the air around us, ready to poison you the moment you take a deep breath."

I could see Noel was really working himself up, and there was very little I could say that was going to do any good. All I could think of was a feeble-sounding remark. "You really sound upset, Noel. You really do."

"Upset?" Noel was practically screaming when he answered. "Upset is putting it mildly. I can't stand him, Jeb. You just can't win with the guy. Unless of course you do everything exactly his way. But that leaves out just about everything that has anything to do with being human."

I have to admit I felt relieved when I heard the phone start to ring. Then Pete came barging into Noel's room to tell me, all breathless and excited like he knew he was bringing really big, important news, "Guess who's home from Florida and calling her boyfriend on the telephone?"

7

We decided to go to Lumpy's for ice cream. We could've met at Stevie's house, but everyone was busy unpacking from Florida, and Stevie said she'd rather meet somewhere else. She could've come over to my house, but with everyone hanging around and the air-conditioning off, that didn't seem too good an idea either. So we agreed on Lumpy's, which is just about halfway between our two houses.

As I was leaving the house, I called back, "See you guys later. I'm going for a bike ride."

I heard Pete say, "No, he's not. He's going to meet his girlfriend at Lumpy's."

The ride from my house to Lumpy's is really easy and

nice. We live on Overlook Road, which is high up on a hill. Route 309 runs down below. In the winter when the trees have no leaves, you can see all the cars go by, but in summer you can't see a thing. You'd think there were no other houses or roads around.

My parents chose the house in summer, and Dad once said that if the real estate agent had showed them the place in the winter, they'd never have bought it.

I like it pretty much all year round. And it doesn't bother me if we see cars in the winter. In fact, the change is kind of neat. When friends come over who haven't been here in the winter, they're always amazed to see Route 309 so close.

So the trip to Lumpy's is mostly downhill. But getting home's really tough, because Overlook gets very steep up where we live. When it snows, kids from all over come to the hill to go sledding, and runners in the area call it Wakefield's "Heartbreak Hill." Lots of people who are training for the New York Marathon make a point of working out on Overlook so they can get in shape for the real Heartbreak Hill.

It was beginning to cool down a little by the time I got going on my bike, and coasting fast down Overlook I got a really good stiff breeze on my face.

Stevie looked great from her vacation in Florida. She was tanner than I've ever seen her, and her hair looked lots lighter from all the sun. She even got some freckles on her nose and face. It was so unbelievably great seeing her again and being with her. At first we were so excited we kept interrupting each other and not finishing sentences or really saying anything that made any sense.

There was so much to say, so much time to catch up on and make up for. Basically her time in Florida was fun, but when I said, "I hope you didn't have *too* much fun," Stevie admitted that she missed me a lot.

Finally we just kind of relaxed and got into the ice cream, and that made it easier, having something kind of immediate to do that we were sharing. The ice cream was delicious. We had three different flavors: Peanut Butter Brickle, Watermelon, and Summer Delight. The Watermelon tasted a little like raspberry sherbet instead of watermelon, but that's OK with me. I love raspberry.

"I bet they just change the labels on some of these flavors to make it look like they've got a huge variety of different ones," Stevie said. She looked cute eating the ice cream, like she was starving and hadn't had a bite to eat in days.

"Didn't your grandparents feed you down in Florida?" I teased her.

She laughed. "Nothing but sun and surf. That's all we got to eat for two straight weeks."

"I bet," I told her and pinched her around the waist to show her I didn't think she was exactly down to bare bones.

"Hey, you're tickling me," she said, but I knew she liked it because she slid a little closer to me in the booth where we were sitting together. "How do you think they make the Summer Delight?" Stevie asked me.

"I think how they do it," I said, "is that they go out and find a girl as beautiful as you are, and they put her through a blender and serve her up as Summer Delight."

"I bet," Stevie said, and laughed like she was a little embarrassed by what I'd just said. "No, really, Jeb, how do you think they make it?"

"I don't know. What do you think?"

"Maybe they actually take lots of different fruit-flavored ice creams they've already made and combine them." Stevie was eating spoonfuls of ice cream in between words. "So you end up with a flavor that has, say, some strawberry in it, some peach, and some of this other stuff that's green." She picked up a spoonful of the green part of Summer Delight and stuck it in my mouth.

"Slime," I said with my mouth full of ice cream. "It's called Slime."

"Lime, idiot, not slime. But what about this other stuff they put in it? The lumpy stuff?"

"I bet they toss in a whole bunch of fresh fruits, but they pulverize them in the blender so you can't tell what you're eating anymore. Bananas, cherries, green grapes. Hey, maybe that's what the green is, grape, made from those real sweet ones with no seeds."

"Did anyone ever tell you you were a genius, Jeb Gray? You have phenomenal powers of deductive logic! I mean, to figure that out about the hunks of fruit, that's really Nobel-prize-winning thinking."

"Hey, you deserve half the prize, Stevie. You were the one who came up with the brilliant hypothesis about the recycling of leftover fruit flavors in the development of Summer Delight ice cream."

"Well, when we win the Nobel for our Theory of Ice Cream, I think we should share the money with Lumpy's.

We could give them some of the prize money as a grant, to further the cause of creating new and better ice-cream flavors."

"I'll go with that on one condition," I told her. "If they give us free ice cream for the rest of our lives."

"A deal," Stevie said, and stuck her hand across to me so we could shake on it, only it was her left hand, because she was still busy shoveling ice cream in her mouth with the right one. We started laughing so hard that people were actually turning around and looking at us.

"Let's get out of here," I whispered to her. "It's getting embarrassing."

We decided to bike back toward Stevie's house but not to go in right away. We left our bikes up on the road a little, and headed down toward Cedar Brook, which runs behind their house in a really nice wooded area.

As we walked I told Stevie about Noel's blockhouse scheme and how he wants me to go along with him.

"I think it's dumb, Jeb, really dumb," was all she said.

I said, "I think so too," but then I really didn't want to talk about it anymore.

"You're not seriously considering doing it, are you, Jeb?" Stevie sounded like she couldn't in a million years imagine such a thing.

"I don't know," I said. "I haven't really made up my mind."

I wanted to drop the subject and was sorry I even brought it up, but obviously Stevie wasn't ready to let go of it yet.

"Jeb, why on earth would you even give a thought to doing a thing like that? Unless it's just a matter of not being able to say no to your brother."

It rankled me when she said that, because I know Stevie doesn't have the highest opinion of Noel, and suddenly I was feeling defensive about him. "I'm not afraid of saying anything I want to Noel, but it's my problem, not yours, and I really don't feel like talking about it anymore."

Stevie looked a little surprised, but she didn't say anything, so I know she could tell I was annoyed. By then we were at the edge of Cedar Brook, and I took Stevie's hand and tugged at it until we were sitting close together by the stream. You can't really even call it a stream, much less a brook, these days. With the drought it's more like a mud trickle. But because of all the tall trees and vegetation, it's a lot cooler than anywhere else.

"Peace?" I asked her after a couple of minutes.

"Peace," she said and squeezed my hand.

When I looked at Stevie she was looking away, up toward the sky, and the outline of her jaw looked like someone had sketched it. Stevie's really beautiful—not pretty in a conventional kind of way, but really beautiful. It's her softness, and the way her skin always shines.

"How does it feel to be beautiful, Stevie?" I asked her.

"I'm not beautiful, Jeb. Not at all. So I don't know how it feels."

"Are you kidding? You're the most beautiful girl I've ever seen."

Stevie scrunched up her nose and shook her head. "Oh, come on, Jeb—"

"But you *are* beautiful, you really are," I told her, as seriously as I could.

"I don't feel like I am. My nose is too broad. My hair

falls too flat. Anyway, there are more important things—at least for me—than being beautiful."

She started to get up then, but I grabbed her arm and tugged her back down. "That's not the point. You *are* beautiful, Stevie. And you should feel that way. It's a waste if you don't feel you're something special when you are."

"What do you mean, 'a waste'?" Stevie said. "Not thinking I'm pretty isn't exactly the same as leaving food on your plate with all the poor starving children in India."

And then she got quiet and serious. When she started to talk again, it sounded like she was talking about something completely different and unrelated.

"When I was a little girl, I had very long hair, even longer than I have now. My mother didn't like my long hair because she said it always looked messy. But I liked the way it felt. I don't think I really even cared then so much how it looked. I just liked the feel of it. It kind of kept me company and made me feel secure, especially at night in the wintertime when my room was dark and cold. I always pulled the covers up real close under my chin, and then I'd spread out my hair so it covered my ears and part of my cheeks. My hair always kept me cozy and warm that way.

"Then one day my mother said, 'We're going for a haircut today, Stephanie.' I always hated it when she called me Stephanie instead of Stevie. Anyway, my mother said we had to get my hair cut so it wouldn't look so scruffy all the time. I started to protest and then I started to cry and then I was actually having a fighting, kicking, screaming fit. It's the only time I can ever remember having a real live temper tantrum like that. Oh, except maybe the time I broke my pedometer. But that was a whole other thing that had to do with when Daddy died last year. I was angry that he wasn't around to give me the present he chose for me.

"What did your mother do?" I asked her. It was really hard for me to imagine Mrs. Farr, who seems so reasonable and calm whenever I see her, causing a fit like that about a simple thing like hair.

"What did my mother do? She did what she always does. She went right ahead and carried out her plan to get my scruffy, messy, ugly hair cut!"

I reached out and held Stevie then. I pulled her in close to me, with her head turned sideways on my shoulder. I smoothed the long strands of her hair over her ears and over her cheeks until she didn't seem angry anymore.

I felt this tremendous desire to protect her, and then another, different kind of feeling began. It was really powerful when it hit me, but something made me hold back. It just didn't seem like the kind of moment to do anything together. I mean anything close and sexual like I wanted to do.

I had to kind of think myself away from the feeling, because the longer I held Stevie, the harder it was to hold back. I don't know why exactly, but the image of a summer field of wheat came into my mind, and then I got a picture of sunlight over a deep blue sea, and then I was thinking really hard, pretending in my head that I was off somewhere safe and beautiful with Stevie, somewhere where she would feel all happy and good again, with me.

I reached my hand out and placed my finger over her

mouth. I left it there for a moment, feeling the softness of Stevie's skin. Before I took it away, I felt her lips kind of whisper a kiss, more of a breath than an actual kiss, but I felt her lips move against my finger, and the feeling it gave was gentler than anything I've ever felt before.

After a while Stevie stood up, shook her hair loose like she was shaking herself loose from her memories, and said in a normal-sounding voice, "Well, anyway, that was a long time ago, and this is now, and my hair is long again, the way I like it."

"I can't imagine your mother doing that, Stevie," I told her. "Why did your haircut matter so much to her?"

"It didn't matter to her. That's just it, Jeb. It mattered to me, not to her."

"But then why would she insist? Especially when you resisted so hard?" I wanted to know.

"Because my mother didn't understand."

All I could think of saying was, "You must really hate your mother for doing that."

"I used to hate her for it when I was younger," she said, "but I don't anymore. I understand how she misunderstood me, and I guess I can accept it because I know she really loves me, even though she sometimes lets me down. Everyone lets the people they're close to down sometimes. Just because a person doesn't do everything you want doesn't mean you don't love them, Jeb."

I was still thinking that over when Stevie started talking again.

"You know what I think? I think the reason you're not sure that you want to say no to Noel about that ridiculous blockhouse scheme of his is because you're afraid that if you let him down he won't love you anymore, or he'll think *you* don't care about *him* anymore."

I started to say, "I don't know about that—" but Stevie interrupted me.

"You know how you were saying before that it's a waste if someone has something special and doesn't realize it? Well, I think it's a waste if someone who's special acts like he's not."

"What do you mean?" I asked.

"I mean exactly what I said, Jeb. You're too special, too good, with too much to offer, to spend your energy on some dumb prank that could land you in one huge heap of trouble."

"I suppose you think I'm better than Noel, more special, or something like that." It came out sounding defensive.

"I didn't say anything of the kind, Jeb, and you know it." Then Stevie's tone of voice changed and got much softer, and she took my hand and said, "All I'm trying to say is that I think you're beautiful too, Jeb. Only I mean on the inside, in your spirit."

"Well," I told her, and I was smiling now, "my beautiful spirit sure is glad your beautiful body came home from Florida."

8

When I got home, it was around eleven o'clock. It looked like everyone was in bed; the house was dark except for the little light in the hall that Mom leaves on all night. But when I got upstairs I saw light coming from under Noel's door, so I figured he might still be up. I went to his door and knocked lightly. I didn't want to disturb him, in case he'd fallen asleep with his light on.

He was listening to some tapes and thumbing through some magazines when I came in, and he looked kind of edgy, like maybe he'd been waiting for me and was annoyed I took so long getting back.

"How ya doing?" I asked him, trying to keep it light.

"Just great, wonderful. Can't you tell? It's just delightful in this steam bath, don't you think?"

To tell you the truth, the house felt OK to me. It had cooled down a lot since the afternoon, and with the windows all open and a little breeze coming through, it didn't feel much different from the air outside, which was comfortable.

"It's not too bad. Better than it would've been last week if the air-conditioning had gone off then."

"I bet you'd think anything was better this week now that what's-her-name's back from California."

"Her name's Stevie, and she wasn't in California. It was Florida." Noel always makes some wisecrack about my relationship with Stevie. I figure he's just jealous, because he never manages to do too well with girls, but it really bugs me when he does it.

"Well, pardon me," Noel said in this real snide voice. "The way you've been moping around these past couple of weeks, I figured she had to be far away."

"I wouldn't exactly say *I've* been the one who's moping around," I told Noel.

"Well, what's to not mope around about? What's there to do in this lousy little hayseed town?" Noel was obviously in one of his self-pitying moods, and whenever he gets like that, I can't stand indulging him.

"Is that why you cooked up this blockhouse scheme? You're bored and have nothing better to do with yourself?" I asked him. Right away I could see the anger flare up in him.

"Hell, no. I'm not going to sit around doing nothing while that jerk Robinson rips everyone off around here. Someone's got to teach him a lesson." Noel crumbled up a torn-out page of the magazine he was looking through when I came in and tossed it against the wall.

"Listen, Noel," I said, sitting down on the edge of his bed, "I've been thinking. . . ."

"That's the problem with you, Jebby: always thinking, never *acting*." Noel sounded like he was prepared for what was coming.

"Look, if you're going to get snotty about this—"

Noel didn't even wait for me to finish. "Don't give me this crap about my getting snotty, Jeb. Just say what you want to say, for Christ's sake, without a whole big buildup."

"OK, if that's what you want, I'll tell it to you straight. I'm not with you on this water-leak thing, and I think you should think twice about doing it yourself. It's risky, and you could land yourself in one huge heap of trouble."

I heard Stevie's words coming out of my mouth and felt a little like a jerk for copying them exactly, but I really did agree with everything she said.

"If you wanna chicken out, go ahead, Jeb. But don't give me some schoolboy lecture on right and wrong. I get enough of that from Father Law in there." Noel hitched his thumb in the direction of Mom and Dad's room. "I can make up my own mind about what I do."

"You can also wind up making a big mistake," I told him and started to walk toward the door.

Noel jumped up and grabbed my arm. "Don't threaten me, Jeb. I'm warning you, don't threaten me."

I pulled away from him and looked at him real hard and straight. It was scary, seeing his face all twisted up with anger. Half of me wanted to punch him out, and half of me felt pity for the guy. I just couldn't figure where all the anger in him kept coming from, and I felt helpless to stop it—or, for that matter, to stop him from doing this thing to Robinson. Then an idea flashed across my mind.

"You know what I think, Noel? I don't think you're really getting back at Robinson for wasting other people's water. I think you're getting back at yourself for messing up your own life."

As soon as I got in my own room, I had this sinking sensation. It felt like I was losing my brother as my friend. I kept thinking about what Stevie had said about how you don't stop loving a person because they let you down, but I just knew that for Noel things worked differently. I mean, Noel's the kind of person who *could* stop loving or liking a person because that person wouldn't go along with him. I went to bed with a really heavy feeling that something awful was happening or was about to happen, and I knew it had to do with turning Noel down.

9

Noel kept pretty much to himself for the rest of the weekend, and I was out with Stevie practically the whole time, so nothing much else got said between him and me.

On Sunday night Mom reminded us that Aunt Nell was having her annual Labor Day picnic, and all Noel said when Mom asked if he'd be coming along was, "I'll skip, thanks." Dad made a face like he wasn't too pleased and said, "We'll see about that, Noel." Mom shot him a look which meant, Cool it for now, so Dad didn't launch into his usual lecture on how Noel is part of the family and should act accordingly, et cetera, et cetera.

Aunt Nell and Uncle Al live in Bridgewater, the next town over, and ever since I was little, they've always invited a whole crowd of family and friends to spend Labor Day around their pool. They've got four kids—our cousins Steve, Allison, Amy, and Benjy, who each invite their own friends—so there are always tons of kids.

I asked Mom if she thought it'd be OK to invite Stevie, and she said it would be fine. Stevie and I made plans to pick her up around noon.

When I woke up this morning, Labor Day, I could tell right away it was going to be one of those scorching hot days. Even as early as nine o'clock, you could feel the heat hit you like a wall as soon as you stepped outside.

Noel slept through breakfast. When Mom sent me up to tell him we were all ready to leave for Aunt Nell's, he just mumbled that he wasn't coming and to leave him alone so he could get some sleep.

When I went back down and told Mom, Dad was standing there loading up a shopping bag with some food, and he said in a real steady, even voice, "If Noel doesn't want to join us, that's his choice." I figured he and Mom had had a talk about how they were going to handle it.

Just as we were about to leave, Mom called for Pete. He'd been helping load potato chips and stuff a few minutes before, but now we didn't see him anywhere.

"Could you look for him, Jeb?" Mom called. "And please, make it fast so we can get going."

I looked around on the first floor and then I started upstairs, calling his name. When I got to the top of the landing, there he was, sitting in front of Noel's closed door, his arms wrapped tight around his knees.

"Hey, Slowpoke, whatcha doin'?" I asked him, but Pete just sat there, not saying anything.

I could hear Mom complaining about how late we would be if we didn't leave soon.

"Come on, Pete, don't you want to get there so we can all go swimming?"

"I don't want to get anywhere, and I hate swimming in Aunt Nell's pool. It's too wet and slimy." Pete's voice was muffled, because he had his head stuck down over his knees so I couldn't see his face.

"What do you mean, their pool's too wet? How can water be too wet, you goon?" I was trying to humor him a little so he'd get moving, but he obviously wasn't in the mood for that.

"And besides," Pete was saying, "I'm spending today with Noel working on the cicadas."

"Oh, no, you're not, young man." Dad was on the landing behind me now. "You're coming with us, and you're coming right this minute."

Dad was standing over Pete now, and in an instant he had wrapped a hand around Pete's arm and stood him straight up on his feet. Pete didn't say anything more—I guess he knew he wasn't going to get his way—just kind of reluctantly dragged along next to Dad, down the stairs and out to the car. It was really pathetic the way he looked, like a criminal being taken prisoner.

I guess because I was looking forward to picking Stevie up and to getting to the picnic, which is always lots of fun, I really forgot to think about Noel and what he was planning to do. Somewhere in the back of my brain I knew what he had in mind, but that morning as we were getting everything ready to go, I kept myself too busy to think about it.

Stevie looked great when she came out of her house and ran to the car. She was wearing a pair of red running shorts with an L.A. Olympics T-shirt. As she came out to the car, she was carrying a pair of running shoes, which she hadn't had time to put on before we came. I got this proud feeling as Mom and Dad said hello to her. I know they like Stevie a lot and think she's a really nice girl. Pete likes her a lot too, because she's always real nice to him and asks him lots of questions about all the stuff he's interested in. She's good at getting along with little kids because she has a younger brother, Robby, and I guess she's had a lot of experience from dealing with him. The moment Stevie got in the car, Pete began to perk up.

The picnic was terrific. The minute—I mean, *the* minute—we arrived, Pete charged off to the pool and did a big cannonball right into the middle of a bunch of our cousins' friends. I don't think Pete got out of the pool once all day, except toward the end when Uncle Al started slicing down the watermelon. So much for wet and slimy water.

Stevie just fit right in like one of the gang. Our cousins had a lot of kids over, as usual, so it was really like one big pool party and barbecue, with parents and other adults around. Stevie and my cousin Amy, who's also going to be a sophomore next year, hit it off really well. At one point I couldn't find Stevie anywhere, and when she finally showed up again, she told me she'd been up in Amy's room talking for about half an hour.

Later on, after dinner, Amy came over and said to me, "You've got a nice girlfriend, Cuz." Then she winked real big at me and said, "I can't imagine what she sees in you, though."

It was practically sundown when we left Aunt Nell's, and everyone was stuffed to the brim from barbecued chicken and ribs and watermelon. As we were leaving, Uncle Al gave me a real big hearty handshake.

"I hear you turned out to be not so dumb after all. Your dad tells me you have a shot at Yale."

I kind of stuttered around for a moment and then mumbled something like, "Yeah, well, we'll have to see, Uncle Al."

"Any thoughts about what you're going to take up when you get there?" Uncle Al asked. "Think you might follow the old man's example and go into the law?"

"I don't think so, Uncle Al," I told him. "I think I'll leave the law to Dad."

After about a million goodbyes, we all piled into the car and headed home. Stevie and I had the back of the car to ourselves because Pete was sitting up front between Mom and Dad. I had that peaceful, exhausted feeling you get from being outdoors all day. Pete convinced Dad to play his favorite station on the radio, and I remember kind of half hearing a nice slow number by Kenny Rogers. I looked up at one point, and we were driving right into the sunset, which was really beautiful. Kind of quiet and still the way sunset in the country is when no one much is around. The sky was all streaked with lavender-blue and pink-orange stripes. It must've been eight thirty already, but there was still enough light in the sky to see everything. Sundown doesn't come till almost nine, even though we're past the high point of summer.

Somewhere toward the end of the drive home, when I was dozing off on Stevie's shoulder, a news bulletin suddenly came on. They kept saying the word "bulletin, bulletin, bulletin, bulletin," over and over again. I woke up with a start and saw Dad, who was driving, lean forward to turn up the volume. By the time the message came over the radio, I was wide awake.

Apparently vandals have entered a blockhouse control-ling the water supply to Northport, part of Ellenville, Roslyn, Wakefield, and Wessex. It appears that in open-ing a valve at the Notamiset aqueduct, a chain reaction has been set in motion which has caused the flooded blockhouse to collapse and huge pipelines to burst, cut-ting off Northport from its water supply. . . .

I felt instantly frozen, like a huge ice cast had just been placed over my whole body. But somehow, through the frozen feeling, my thoughts were clear. At least at first. The bulletin went on to give details, and I remember how specific the figures they gave were. I even remember think-ing, How can they know so much so soon?

The bulletin told how more than a thousand feet of two forty-eight-inch mains were torn away after "rupturing." That was the word they used, "rupturing." I remember it exactly because I got an image of a huge ruptured artery, like in one of those model hearts they have in the biology lab at school.

The radio was telling how tens of millions of gallons of water were crashing down the hillside, how trees were collapsing, houses were being evacuated, and mud slides and gushing water were cutting a ravine in the hillside "one thousand feet long" and "one hundred feet deep and wide."

I don't know how it's possible, but I remember the exact numbers. Kind of like the way a reader with a photographic memory remembers all the words on a page. I wonder if there's such a thing as photographic hearing.

Mayor Gillespie of Northport was saying that the cost of repairs would be in the millions.

I just sat there, not moving and maybe not even breathing, as the meaning of the message sunk in. It didn't happen slowly, but with sudden absolute impact. It came to me all at once, the whole monstrous proportion of the disaster. I could visualize the rocky hillside and the small, solid cement blockhouse, and I saw in my mind the gushing water and the muddy land with deep ruts like gashes running through it.

It was so clear, like a movie happening right in front of me. At first I'd see the hillside and the blockhouse as I remembered them, and then I'd imagine them collapsed and destroyed. They flashed like frames of filmstrip, first one, then the other, over and over again in my mind.

But I couldn't place Noel in the picture. Where was he now? Hurt somewhere and hidden? Home and safe? The bulletin didn't mention who did it, just that it was done by vandals. If they thought there was a group of them, then they couldn't know that it was just Noel. So Noel must be safe. At least for now. But he must be scared, scared to death. I could feel his fear as though it were my own. And then I thought the inevitable thought behind all the others: It could've been me, too.

I sat there in the back of the car frozen in panic. I didn't even want to look at Stevie, who was right there next to me, because I was afraid I'd let on that we knew something. And Stevie didn't turn her head to look at me. At some point during the bulletin she must've reached over and held my hand, but I don't remember when. I just remember looking down after a while and seeing our two clasped hands there, but I couldn't feel either one of them.

My mind raced through a million possibilities of where Noel could be, but there was no way of knowing, and no way to hurry the time until I could find out. I felt trapped riding in the car and had to fight back the urge to bolt outside and start running. Not that I could've gotten anywhere if I had, but that's how I felt, like running for my life. My heart was beating so fast and so hard that I was sure everyone in the car could hear it.

The bulletin kept returning like a buzz saw in the background that someone is turning on and off. It felt like someone was fiddling with the volume knob, spinning it back and forth, but the spinning was inside me.

Officials are saying that if Northport cannot restore a steady water source within five days, parts of Northport will run out of water. A heat wave that pushed temperatures today into the mid-nineties is expected to increase water use and has heightened the officials' concern. . . .

I could only get a rough idea, in the state I was in, of the emergency plans that were being made to replace pipelines, to borrow water, to limit water use. The information was coming too fast now. I felt bombarded and couldn't get hold of it.

Everything sounded enormous, too huge to comprehend. Tens of tons. Thousands of feet. Millions of gallons. It was losing all meaning to me. None of the details were sticking anymore. Just the impact, like a huge, immovable cement block.

But somehow, through it all, one thing was absolutely clear. It felt like I'd crossed some great watery divide between two lands or continents. I knew, just knew, that nothing would ever be the same again. Then I remember Dad saying something, reacting, and I could feel myself really breathe for the first time since the bulletin came on.

"My God," Dad was saying, "this is unbelievable. It's the driest summer in history. My God, this is insane. Whoever did it deserves ten years in prison!"

When Dad said that, the idea that Noel had actually broken a law for which he could be tried and sentenced came to me for the first time. Then the radio was reporting more information:

The blockhouse is situated on a bluff of a wooded hill within the Notamiset's one-hundred-thirty-five-acre Mountainview Park. Officials have said there are about thirty such blockhouses within the Northport watershed, all containing air-pressure valves, along the Notamiset aqueduct's thirty-two-mile route between Northport's five reservoirs and the storage reservoir in Cedar Grove. The only security for the blockhouses has been padlocks on manhole covers leading into them.

I remember hearing one of the Northport officials make the statement, "You'd need an entire army to patrol all the right of way." And I was thinking, when he said it, how no one ever went anywhere near the blockhouse. Not once in all the time Noel and I had spent on that desolate hillside did we ever see another soul.

Who could've ever imagined that what was actually happening could have happened? A little stream of escaping water was all Noel pictured. Not some wild tidal wave destroying homes and threatening lives!

Then I felt a sharp, searing pain in my stomach, and I knew I was going to be sick. I called to Dad to stop the car quick and barely made it out. It seemed like I was vomiting forever there on the side of the road. I didn't think I'd eaten that much in my whole entire life. I was so weak when it was over that I could barely stand.

Dad was there next to me, holding me around my shoulders as I stood cold and shaking. "Come on, son, we'd better get you home," he said, and then he kind of steered me back toward the car.

Dad kept the radio off for the rest of the trip home. I remember Pete saying, "Jeb shouldn't've pigged out on so much chicken and ribs," and then the only sound was gears changing and the car engine turning over.

—10—

Everything happened remarkably fast after that. The details are a blur, but the basic facts are clear.

Dad stopped at Stevie's house first. When she said good-bye, she leaned into the back window and squeezed my hand and said in a scared-sounding whisper, "Call me later, Jeb. For sure."

I think I mumbled, "Promise," but I can't remember.

As soon as we walked into our house, the phone started ringing. Or maybe it was already ringing when we opened the door. It was Dad who picked the phone up, and the moment I heard him say, "Yes, this is Mr. Gray, Noel's father," I knew the police had Noel.

When Dad got off the phone, he turned to Mom.

"It's about Noel. Seems he's gotten into some trouble and they have him down at the station house. I'll handle this, Laura. You stay here with Pete and Jeb."

But before Mom could say anything, I said, " I'm coming too. I know what it's about, and I'm coming too, Dad."

I guess I was expecting him to object, and it came as a surprise when all Dad said was, "Help me unload the car, Jeb, and then we'll leave right away."

"What'd Noel do, Dad?" Pete was asking, but Mom said something to him about our not really knowing, and then she led him out of the room.

The ride to the station house takes about five minutes from where we live, but it seemed much longer than that. As soon as we turned out of the driveway, Dad asked me, not even looking at me but with his eyes still on the road in front of him, "What's it about, Jeb?"

I had to overcome my sense of betraying Noel to tell Dad, but I knew I had to warn him of what was coming.

"Dad, this is going to be—" I started to tell him, but he interrupted me in a voice that sounded ice cold with anger.

"Just give it to me straight, Jeb. What's he done?"

"Oh, God," I began, and then I started to shake all over and sobbed the words out: "It's the Northport reservoir flood we heard on the radio. . . ."

All Dad said then, and for the rest of the drive to the station house, was, "I'm going to kill that kid. I'm going to kill him."

I spent the rest of the drive fighting down nausea. Even though it was still really hot and humid, I was chilled all over. I knew it was because I was really scared.

When we got to the station house, Dad pulled the car around back where you're supposed to park, but all the places were filled with squad cars, so we had to back out and find a place on the street. Dad's face had an angry, closed expression, and I didn't dare say a word the whole time he was looking for a parking spot.

The Wakefield police station is really just a converted old house on Main Street. It looks just like any other house, except that the front door, which is white, has POLICE written in big black letters across it.

When we walked into the station house, the place was mobbed. I recognized a couple of Wakefield cops, like Officer MacDougal and Sergeant Scott, and then there were a bunch of cops from someplace else plus some guys dressed in regular street clothes who looked like maybe they were detectives or something.

One of the guys in plain clothes—a big fat guy with a cigarette hanging out of his mouth as he talked—put his hand on my chest as I came through the door and kind of pushed me back and said, "What do you want, kid? They're questioning someone inside and don't want to be disturbed."

I felt like punching him in the nose, but Dad, who was right behind me, stepped between us and told the fat guy he was Noel's father.

The fat guy turned and announced real loud, "The father of the juvenile they're holding inside has arrived. Tell the Chief."

It sounded weird calling Noel a "juvenile." I mean he's sixteen, almost seventeen years old. But I know that's what they call minors who get arrested.

Sergeant Scott must've been listening to the whole conversation, because he came over to Dad and said, "Hello, Mr. Gray. I'm afraid there's been some trouble—big trouble—and they're holding Noel for questioning."

Sergeant Scott looked sad as he said it, so I could tell that the whole situation was really heavy.

"Can I see my son now?" Dad asked. His voice was unsteady.

"I'm afraid not right now, Mr. Gray. Not until they complete the preliminary questioning," Sergeant Scott told him. "But I'll let Chief Warren know you're here."

"Does the boy have a lawyer in there with him?" Dad sounded like he was about to get real angry and defensive, but Sergeant Scott told him that Noel had waived his right to silence, said he didn't want a lawyer or his parents, and had confessed to breaking into the Northport Watershed just a couple of hours ago.

The fat guy laughed this big loud laugh that sounded like a cackle and said, "Smartass kid thought he'd have himself a private splash party up there at the reservoir. Only problem was, he left his T-shirt at the scene, and it just so happened it has his last name printed clear as day right across the back of it. Kid ain't as smart as he thinks."

I knew instantly which shirt Noel must've been wearing: the blue baseball shirt with *Wakefield Wonders* on the front and GRAY in white iron-on block-print letters across the back.

Then the fat guy blew some smoke circles in another detective's face and said, "Kid must have some kinda death wish."

For a moment I thought Dad was actually going to punch the guy, but Sergeant Scott broke it up by going over to the fat guy and telling him something in a voice I couldn't hear, but which managed to cool him down. Then Sergeant Scott came over to Dad and quietly told him how these guys were from Northport, not Wakefield, and how they can get a little heavy-handed up there. "Try to ignore it, sir," he said to Dad in a whisper, and Dad nodded his head up and down slowly, looking sad and defeated and like he'd suddenly lost his steam.

I was wondering the whole time how Noel could've worn that shirt, of all shirts, to do this thing. And what on earth made him take it off? I figured it was the heat. Noel must've been working hard on getting into the blockhouse. Probably got himself all sweated up and decided to take the shirt off until he finished. Then maybe the flood happened so suddenly that he tore out of there too fast to think of it. I decided that's probably how it happened. Noel must've panicked, or he'd never have left his shirt there for anyone to find.

Officer MacDougal, who lives around the corner from us, came up and said, "Hello, Mr. Gray," to Dad and put his hand on my shoulder in this nice, sympathetic, supportive way.

"How's Noel?" I asked him. My voice sounded weak and wobbly.

"Holding up pretty good, Jeb." Officer MacDougal answered my question, but he was looking at Dad as he spoke. "He kind of cracked awhile back when he first came clean about what he'd done, but that happens to a lot of them. The damage is pretty bad, and a couple of the

Northport police were pretty hard on him for a while there, until he 'fessed up."

"This is pretty serious stuff," the fat guy who'd called Noel a juvenile said. "This ain't child's play."

By then I'd figured out that not only this guy but the other ones I didn't recognize were Northport cops who must've come down to Wakefield when they recovered Noel's shirt. That explained the full parking lot in back.

All of a sudden the door to the back room opened, and Noel came out. Officer Hayes and Chief Warren were leading him, one holding each arm.

Noel saw me right away, all the way across the station house, and smiled a big smile. I could tell he was surprised and then glad to see me. Officer Hayes and Chief Warren led him straight through the crowd of people that were in the room and over to Dad, who was standing a little off to one side, by the window. Chief Warren was saying something quietly to Dad, and Dad was nodding and looking kind of dazed. Then he turned to me and said in a voice that he was obviously trying to control, "You take the car home now, Jeb, and tell your mother I'll call her shortly."

And Officer Hayes and Chief Warren, followed by Dad, led Noel toward the front door of the station house. Just as they passed by, Noel said to me, "I guess you knew what you were doing, Jeb. Keep in touch, hey?"

I said, "You bet, pal," and then he was gone, out the door.

As I was leaving, the fat guy behind me said, "No more splash parties for that wiseass once he gets to Culver Detention Center."

11

School started on Wednesday, the day after the day after Labor Day. That's how they do it in Wakefield, not like a lot of other places where they start up again on Tuesday, right after Labor Day Monday. Mom always calls the extra day a "day of grace," at least she usually does. But since the thing with Noel happened, she mostly just does what's necessary to get through each day. She doesn't seem to have too much interest or energy for humor anymore, so I didn't hear her say anything about our "day of grace" this year.

Mom let me have the car on Tuesday to get some things I needed before school started. I was amazed when I saw how much my feet had grown over the summer. The last pair of track shoes I bought, my Saucony Shadows, was in June, and those were nine and a half. This time I needed an eleven.

It's only Monday now: the first Monday of the first full week of senior year, which seems endlessly long now that it's finally here but has hardly begun.

Last Monday seems like a million years ago. Like some great divide got crossed since then, separating one part of my life from the rest of it. Noel's in Culver Juvenile Detention Center, where they took him right from the station house, and no one has any idea how long they're going to keep him there.

I think Mom and Dad must've made some kind of pact not to talk about it in front of me and Pete anymore. After they came back from visiting Noel last week, Dad said that it can be weeks and in some cases even months before juveniles being held at places like Culver get a hearing, and that the authorities have the right to keep them there until then. Mom told Pete, "Dad is doing everything he can, both as Noel's father and as a lawyer, to help hurry the process of getting Noel home to us."

And that was the last either of them had to say. You kind of get the feeling around here that nothing happened at all, or that something happened that's too horrible to even remember. It feels almost as though we once had another person in the house, and he died of some unspeakably awful disease, so we buried him and made a deal to pretend he never existed.

The worst part of what happened, which no one even heard about until late Monday night, was that Robinson's house was destroyed in the flood. Absolutely destroyed, wiped out, gone for good. That's how forceful the flooding was. Robinson's house was right down at the bottom of the hill from the blockhouse, so the water just washed it away. That sure isn't going to help Noel's hearing, when it comes.

When I got home from school today, there was a letter for me from Noel, which Mom left out on the kitchen table, where she always leaves my mail. Judging from Noel's letter, Culver sounds like a pretty dismal place to be holed up in.

The letter wasn't dated, so I couldn't figure out exactly when he wrote it and how long it took to get here. But the way the letter sounded, it didn't make much difference what day he wrote it. You got the impression one day's exactly like the next in there.

Noel's not the kind of person who likes writing, and the letter he wrote was six whole pages on a yellow legal pad, so I knew just from the length of it, before I even read what he wrote, that Noel must be dying of boredom. Here's what he had to say:

Dear Jeb,

It's funny how since I'm in this place, I do a lot more thinking and remembering than I ever did before. I guess that's because there's not much to do or much to think about here. It's dull and boring and always the same and real depressing all the time.

I may have sounded negative about my life before, but I take it all back—every single word I ever said about school being bad or the summers being boring—now that I'm locked up in this dump and can't get out. Until they get around to having a hearing about my case, that is, and God knows when that will be. Or what they'll decide. They may not even let me out. They can send me straight from here to a real prison if they want to.

It's all up to the family court judge who hears my case. The guys here say that some judges are real soft on minors, no matter what they've done, and always give first serious offenders—that's what I am—a second chance. Unless you kill someone or something really bad like that. And then they say some of the judges are real sons-of-bitches, out to show the world how tough they are and how they're going to show us punks who's boss. My luck, I'll get one of them and he'll slap a couple of years on me!

This place has some real creeps in it. There's this one dude you just wouldn't believe. I swear, Jeb, you know how tough the toughest guys at Wakefield are—guys like Charlie Russo—well, this guy makes Charlie look like a featherweight.

Mack—that's his name—he's got muscles from head to foot like Arnold Schwarzenegger, I swear, with tattoos over every square inch of his chest and arms. They call him "Muscle Mountain," and this dude's so incredible, whenever they call him that, he smiles this idiot smile, like he's real pleased, and says, "You betcha, sweetheart, that's Mack, Muscle Mountain."

Mack tells everyone he nearly murdered a guy once in a public men's room. Some queer on junk who made a pass at him. Mack says real proud-like that he stabbed the guy a dozen times and left him in a pool of blood. Heard later on the radio the guy was going to live but couldn't give a description of his assailant because he'd been too high on dope to see straight when it happened.

Mack's in for armed robbery of a diner and supposedly raping a waitress out in back in the parking lot. I don't believe that part, though. I think he just throws it in for effect to impress the other jerks here with what a macho dude he is. Robbed a diner and took the time to rape some broad on the way out? Sure!

You just wouldn't believe this guy, Jeb. He's always saying the same thing over and over again, like he doesn't understand what he's in for. "I ain't no bad dude. I'm just a antisocial individual." Guy's gotta have a brain the size of a pea.

You know what I think about a lot since I'm in here? I think about times when I was just free to come and go, to walk around somewhere in the country, or just lie around talking and dreaming, like on Cow Hill.

The other night I remembered the time I told you that the high point of my life was my birthday and you asked how the day I was born could be the high point of my life. I said things had gone downhill ever since. Well, now when I think back, I realize there were lots of high points, ones I never counted. Like just being free to do what I wanted. Like being on the outside where real life goes on. Or like having a brother around—someone normal who you'd want to be with, not some stupid weirdo like the jerks and junkies in this place.

Anyway, that's all gone now. And one thing I know is, this has got to be the absolute lowest point there is. Or if there's something lower, I haven't found it yet.

They don't allow brothers to visit here. Probably they

92

think you'll smuggle drugs and weapons in. Or maybe they're afraid we'll get ahold of bubble gum and ruin our teeth!

One thing they allow is getting letters. I wouldn't mind hearing from you when you get the time. Let me know how Pete is doing. Is he getting on OK since I left? I'd write him a letter too, but I bet the folks'd just tear it up. So you just say hi to the little guy for me. And if you've got a spare buck, give it to him for me, will you? I'll get it back to you when I get home.

Noel

P.S. If I don't get out of here soon, I may lose the semester. My counselor here—a guy named Jake who tells you right away (and all the time after that) how he was once in trouble with the law when he was a kid— Jake says the high school might make me repeat the semester, because the Wakefield Board of Ed says you have to attend classes to get credit.

I read the letter by myself in my room, but when I went down to the kitchen afterward, there was Mom just sitting there at the kitchen table drinking a cup of coffee.

"How does he sound?" she asked me in a weak whisper of a voice. It was her first mention of Noel since she'd told me and Pete that Dad was doing what he could to help get Noel out of Culver.

Somehow her question made me angry. I guess just having read the letter, and thinking about how awful it must be for Noel, and Mom and Dad's not talking about him or anything for so long, I guess I felt they deserved to be blamed in some way. I had the letter in my back pocket, folded up where I'd put it after reading it, and I pulled it out, almost tore it as I did, threw it down on the table, practically in Mom's coffee cup, and shouted at her, "You can damn well find out how he is for yourself! If it matters to you."

And then I ran out of the house in tears.

12

As soon as I got out the door, after saying that to Mom, I began to feel really down and depressed. I'd been planning on going for a run, but I wasn't dressed for running, and I didn't feel up for that anyway. I wasn't in the mood to bum around the neighborhood and maybe bump into a whole bunch of creeps who might look at me like they felt sorry for me because my brother was a societal outcast, so I walked around to the back of our house and went down to the basement through the old Bilco doors. Even though the weather was nice and I could've left the doors open to let more light in, I closed them up tight after going down a couple of steps. I guess I just wanted to be by myself for a while, without anyone interrupting my lousy mood.

Once I got down there and my eyes adjusted to the lack of light, I saw all of Noel's specimen cases set out along the counters that lined the back of the basement. I went over to them to look a little closer, and I noticed a box of little bugs and stuff sitting out on the counter where Noel always does his work. I figured they were some specimens he hadn't gotten around to sorting and setting in the cases yet.

I saw Noel had just begun to put together a new specimen case from a sheet of plywood and some old wood scraps of quarter-round molding. He'd made little in-between sections, approximately two inches square, and I saw where he'd begun to set one specimen in each square, tacking them down to the wood backing with straight pins. There was a whole pile of the straight pins next to the box of unsorted bugs.

As I was looking at all this careful, clever work Noel had done, I kept thinking of that map he made of the area around the blockhouse. The same kind of precision and planning was involved in both the bug collecting and the mapmaking, I realized, only one had been a harmless, constructive kind of thing, and the other had been a disaster.

I sat there on the stool Noel always sits on, trying to figure how one person—one creative, clever mind like Noel's—could go in two such completely different directions. When I heard a knock on the Bilco doors, I ignored it at first, because it sounded like a falling branch, but then it came again, and then a third time, till I knew it was definitely a knocking, like a person wanting to be let in.

It surprised me a little, because people almost never enter the basement through those doors: only workmen or occasionally me or Noel or my parents to store stuff down below. Most people go down the inside stairs leading from the hall.

So it took three sets of knocks before I got up and went over to see who was there. When I finally got the old rusted doors open again, I didn't see anyone, so I just assumed I was wrong. But something made me go up and look around. When I got to the top step, I saw our dog Hank's tail and the green and white jacket Pete always wears turning around the corner of the house.

"Hey there, Pete, that you?" I called. "Where you off to so fast?" But the jacket disappeared completely. "Hey, wait a minute, kiddo," I called again.

I was running now, and as I turned the corner, I practically barreled into Pete, who was just walking away very slowly, ambling along as though he hadn't even heard me call.

"Hey, where you going so fast? I didn't realize it was you knocking before. You hardly gave me a chance to open those heavy basement doors before you ran away," I told him.

"I wasn't knocking on any doors. And I didn't run away," he said.

"What do you mean, you didn't knock?" I asked him. "Wasn't that you knocking at the basement doors before?"

"Nope. Must've been someone else," Pete said.

"It couldn't have been anyone else, Pete. There's no one else around," I told him.

"Wasn't me," Pete said, in a voice which sounded real defiant.

Then I realized he must've felt embarrassed to have been hanging around knocking for so long. Like maybe he figured I didn't want to be bothered.

"Listen, I don't mind that you were knocking on the door," I said. "It didn't bother me. It just took me a while to get there."

Then suddenly Pete started screaming wildly. "I didn't do it. I didn't do it!" And then he was running away, screaming into the air over his shoulder as he ran, "You liar, it wasn't me!"

I was amazed. I had no idea what happened or what I'd said to make him so wild. It seemed like he'd gone completely crazy. But I knew somehow, without really knowing, that Pete's behavior had to do with Noel's getting in trouble and being away. And then I began to feel bad for this little kid whose only friend practically was an invisible make-believe character with a weird name. I just took off as fast as I could after him.

When I finally caught up with him, I grabbed him in a kind of bear hug from behind, but Pete was like a windmill spinning in the breeze: arms like blades flailing out and chopping at the air and at me.

Of course, my being seventeen, I'm much bigger and stronger than Pete, so I overpowered him easily. One moment Pete was all in motion, and the next it was as though the wind that was powering him had stopped dead still. For a moment I was scared that maybe I'd hurt him.

His arms sank down by his sides, and his whole body went limp. His face was muddy with tears mixed with dirt, and his eyes were red and swollen. It looked to me like he'd been crying for hours.

I was still panting from the run, but I managed to ask him, "Hey, Pete, how would you like to come help me set in place some of the bugs Noel didn't get a chance to sort yet? You know lots more about this stuff than I do."

Pete looked up at me with this searching kind of look. Then his smudgy little face broke into a big open smile. "You mean it? Really? You think we should do that, even though . . ." He hesitated a moment, and then repeated, "Even though . . ." but he just couldn't manage to say what I knew was on his mind: even though Noel's not here.

"Sure I mean it," I told him. "I wouldn't've suggested it if I didn't mean it. I think Noel'll appreciate our help . . . when he gets home."

We did our best sorting the loose specimens, naming them as best we could by matching them with other specimens that were already sorted and named, and then fastening them into their individual compartments.

At one point Pete came across the cicada casing he found for Noel that day he was doing his blind-man act and walked into a tree. He matched it to one of the insect specimens and announced with great authority, "This kind's called *Magicicada septendecim*." He separated each syllable out real clearly as he pronounced the words, which he was reading from another case filled with specimens that Noel had already labeled.

"Wow, that's pretty impressive, Pete," I told him. "How'd

you know that? And what the heck does it mean, anyway?"

"It's the Latin name for what dumb people who don't know anything call the 'seventeen-year locust.' But they're not locusts, they're really cicadas. Look at all the neat stuff you can see if you look real close."

Pete grabbed a magnifying glass that was lying on the counter.

"I forget why they call them 'seventeen-year' cicadas," Pete was saying. "I remember Noel telling us the reason that day when I found him the cicada shell, but I forget what the reason was. Do you remember, Jeb?"

"Didn't it have something to do with how long it takes the babies—I think they're called nymphs—to develop into adults?" I asked him.

"Yeah, that's right, I think," Pete said. "But what do they do in the meantime? I forget what he said about how they use up seventeen years getting ready. Do they stay inside an egg or something?"

Then it started to come back to me, the things Noel explained about how the female cicada lays its eggs in tiny slits in the bark or wood of twigs.

"Oh, yeah, now I remember," Pete said, sounding excited, like it was all coming back to him too. "After a while the eggs hatch into nymphs. And they drop from the trees where they're hatched, go down into the ground, and build a cell where the nymph lives for seventeen years, sucking up sap from the roots of trees."

As Pete said the word "cell," I got an image of a prison cell and thought of Noel.

Just when I was thinking this, Pete said, "Like where they're keeping Noel, in a jail cell."

It was a little like ESP, but I didn't know exactly how I should react, so I explained to Pete that the place where they're keeping Noel is called a "detention center," not a jail.

"It's the same thing," Pete said. He sounded real sure of himself. "It's a jail, all right. If it wasn't a jail, Noel'd walk right out of that place and come home."

I guess I didn't know what to say then, so I asked Pete, "Hey, what happens after the nymphs spend seventeen years underground? Do you remember what comes next?"

"They come out as grown-up cicadas. Noel said the whole purpose of their coming out finally is to feed other bugs and things that live off them," Pete said. "He called it 'nature's design.' "

"I guess the poor cicadas don't get much chance to plan their lives," I told Pete.

Then Pete said something which really took me by surprise. "Noel didn't get to plan things, either. They just came and took him away and didn't care if he was finished living yet."

"He's not finished living, Pete," I told him. "He's just off waiting for a hearing."

"Yeah, sure." Pete sounded real sarcastic. "But soon he'll be finished living. They'll just decide he should be dead and then they'll kill him."

I was so shocked that all I could think of to say was, "Pete! Don't say that!"

"I'll say whatever I think, 'cause it's true," Pete said.

I realized I'd made him angry, so I tried to explain.

"Look, Pete, Noel didn't do anything they can kill him for. What he did is something you can be put in jail awhile for, at most, or made to pay a fine maybe. That's all they can do to him for what he did."

Pete's face was red and angry, and there were tears in his eyes, making them look bright and wild.

"Noel didn't do anything. They just said he did it. It's all a lie. He didn't do it, and they're lying, lying, lying. . . ."

Pete was screaming the words now, and crying as he screamed. I had the feeling of being in deeper than I could handle, the same way I felt when Pete went wild screaming before and ran away from me. I wondered how he could really believe Noel didn't cause the blockhouse accident. Was it possible that Pete really thought Noel had been framed?

Everyone knew the truth. Noel had admitted everything, confessed the whole thing.

I looked at Pete's serious little face, and it looked too small inside all his tossed and tangled blond curls. The same wheat color as Noel's hair, only Noel's is completely straight. Pete had a wounded expression on his face, and he looked weak enough for the slightest wind to blow him over.

"Don't you know Noel admitted that he started the flood?" I asked him. "I thought for sure you'd know that. Everyone knows it."

"Well, I don't, 'cause it's not true. I don't care what everyone believes," Pete said. "Noel didn't do it. They're just saying he did. Like when the Devlin twins set off the fire alarm at school last year. They laid that on Noel too.

And when kids were letting air out of tires and stealing parts and stuff off bikes, they said Noel was doing that too. It's all a big fat frame-up. Everyone always says Noel's bad, but it's a lie."

I remembered the times Pete was talking about. "That's different, Pete. Those times Noel was blamed when he didn't do anything. You're right about those times. But this is different. This time Noel did something wrong and admitted it."

Pete was still being stubborn. "I never heard him say he did it. They're all lying just like the other times."

"Listen, Pete," I told him, "I know Noel did this, because he told me he did it. But what happened was an accident. Noel didn't *mean* to make anything like this happen."

For the first time I could see that Pete was letting my words seep in a little, beginning to turn over some new possibilities in his head.

When he finally spoke again, Pete started in real slow and careful, like he wanted to be sure he could trust the situation before he went too far. "You mean the flood was an accident instead of on purpose?"

"That's what I mean," I said, "and that's the truth. Noel did make it happen, but he didn't mean to. He just meant to let a little trickle of water out. Just enough to get old man Robinson's goat. Not to drown out his house and the whole damn hillside."

"Why'd he do that?" Pete asked, and then looked like he shouldn't have. "I mean, if what you're saying's true and all."

"Noel found out that old Potato Head's been filching

water, and he thought it would be kind of a funny way to get back at him. And then the joke got serious and ran away on him."

"Well, if what happened was an accident, then they have to let Noel go free. They can't kill someone for an accident. That's not fair."

I tried to explain. "No, they can't kill Noel for what he did, but according to the law, they do have to look at the results of what a person does. A bad accident can sometimes be the result of playing a prank."

"I don't care what you say, or what anyone else says," Pete told me, and I could tell he'd already made up his mind what he believed and was going to stick with it. "Noel didn't do it. He didn't. I know he didn't."

And then Pete started crying again, and saying over and over, "He didn't do it. . . . He didn't do it."

I realized that Pete just couldn't accept the idea that his big brother could've caused so much damage to anyone or anything. I had nothing left to say, so I just put my hand on his head and kind of rubbed his tangly mess of curls.

Suddenly I remembered about the letter from Noel and his asking me to look after Pete. I reached down in my pocket and pulled out some bills, found a single, and handed it to Pete.

"Hey, I almost forgot. This is from Noel," I told him. "He sent it to me to give to you. He says he misses you a lot."

Pete looked at the dollar bill real hard, and then he grabbed it and ran up the basement steps two at a time and out the Bilco doors.

When I looked up at the sky, I saw that it had gone completely dark. I couldn't see Pete anymore, but I heard him calling, "Come, Hankie, come on, boy. Time to come back home for dinner."

I didn't see Hank, but after a moment I heard Pete say, "Good boy, Hankie. That's a good dog." And then they were gone.

13

It took me a few days to write back to Noel. Each time I thought of writing, I didn't know what to say. Or I'd suddenly feel like doing something else to avoid having to say something. I finally managed a couple of pages. Nothing as long as Noel's letter. Here's what I wrote:

Dear Noel,

Got your letter and was glad to hear from you. I don't know what to say about how awful that place sounds. I just know how awful you must feel being cooped up there and not knowing what the outcome will be.

Things are pretty much the same as always around here. School's OK. Maybe a little tougher than last year, and the college pressure's mounting fast. Applications and all that stuff.

Some kids aren't applying because they plan to work straight out of school when they graduate. Sam Rogers already lined up a job with the township—leaf cleanup and snow plowing and general work like that. He goes around bragging about how he's just coasting his way now until June and graduation. It's a good thing his father's on the Township Committee. Otherwise I doubt that guy could land a job doing anything.

You asked about Pete. I hope you don't mind, but since he seemed like he was missing you a lot, I asked him to help me mount a couple of those bug specimens you left lying around the basement. The kid seems real interested in the stuff and knows a whole lot about it. He says he learned it all from you. I gave him that dollar for you, and he says thanks. He misses you too.

Mike McPherson cracked his dad's Honda up on Silverspring Road going around the bend there by those new condominiums. No one hurt, but everyone in the car had been drinking, and I hear Mike's father's on the warpath. Apparently they were at Pat Storey's house, and her parents were letting everyone drink beer.

Nothing much more to say. Do what you can to get the hell out of there as fast as you can. Not that you're missing much here, but it's got to be better than there.

Jeb.

What can you say to someone whose life looks like it's going down the tubes? The worst part is how guilty I feel being free and on the outside while Noel's locked up in that horrible place. It's hard not to keep thinking, It might've been me.

When I finished the letter and reread what I'd written, it somehow all seemed like lies, or beside the point of what's really happening in my life these days. I was thinking about Stevie and all the good things going on between us and how great it feels waking up every day now, knowing there's something special to look forward to when we'll be together again.

I didn't want to tell Noel how Stevie and I have been out running together practically every day after school, because up until last year and meeting Stevie, Noel was the person who'd run with me lots of times in the afternoons. And even though it wasn't *because* I was running with Stevie that Noel gave up running—he gave it up when he didn't make the team—I know Noel's been resentful of her.

And then I thought about Pete and how sad and lost the little guy seems with Noel away. I sure couldn't tell Noel that in my letter. It'd make him miserable. And I didn't want to go on too much about how happy Pete was when he and I were working on the bugs together; it'd sound like I was trying to take Noel's place.

So instead I just about said nothing, at least nothing really real or important. Just trivial things. But no matter how trivial and un-special I tried to make life on the outside sound, this is home to Noel and Noel is away from home, locked away somewhere ugly and depressing where nothing is normal or trivial anymore.

14

Senior year is getting really hard, much tougher than I thought it'd be. It's not so much the studying that's hard, although the work is pretty rough, and physics is probably the hardest course I've ever taken. But a big part of what makes facing each day at school hard is the way I feel when I'm around all these kids who know about Noel and don't know what to say or how to act with me. And then there's college applications.

It's only October, but I have to get my Yale application in by November first, because I'm applying for "Early Action." That means I'm letting Yale know that I'll accept them if they accept me. And in return for my applying for "Early Action," they save me the agony of waiting until spring to hear if I'm in. I think it's around December fifteenth that the letters go out. It's a good deal, *if* you're pretty sure you want a certain college. You also have to have really top grades for the college advisor at Wakefield, Mrs. Galsworthy, to let you do it.

I guess I want Yale, but sometimes I think I shouldn't go there because my father did. But Yale's a great school, and it'd be dumb to turn down the possibility of going there just because my father went there twenty-five years ago. Stevie says she thinks I'd be spiting myself not to apply, and I agree.

So here I am up to my eyeballs in essay questions about everything you can imagine. There's more darn work writing one of these than writing a term paper, I swear.

At dinner tonight I mentioned how Noel might miss a whole semester of school.

"Why do you have to attend classes to get credit?" I said.

And then little Pete piped up with, "It's 'cause Noel's in jail."

Dad launched into a big lecture on the difference between detention centers and prisons, how a detention center is a kind of "mid-station in the justice system." But the whole time I was thinking that it does the same thing a prison does—keeps you locked away where you can't get at the life you wish you were still living.

Obviously Pete's mind was running on the same track, because after Dad explained the difference, Pete said, in a real stubborn, angry-sounding voice, "It's a jail. Noel's in a jail. If he wasn't in jail, he'd come home."

110

Then Dad tried to explain a little about how the juvenile justice system works, but he didn't get too far before Pete, who obviously wasn't listening to a thing he was saying, interrupted and came out with his theory of how Noel was innocent and had been framed.

"It's all a lie about Noel," Pete said very quietly, almost as though to himself. "He didn't do it. They just said he did, but they're lying."

Mom leaned over and took Pete's hand, but he pulled it away real fast like he wanted her to know he wasn't looking for sympathy.

I wasn't too keen on hearing Dad's lecture either. Noel's been in that place over a month, and just this week his hearing with Judge Coopersmith got scheduled. I found out from Stevie's Uncle Ralph, who's in the county prosecutor's office, that Coopersmith's considered one of the toughest family system judges around. He's the one who sent Jesse Kawalski to the clink.

Thinking about that made me really mad, and I said, "The one thing you can't convince me of is that this so-called juvenile justice system has anything to do with justice. You can't tell me some lousy stinking system is just when it keeps a guy locked up for six weeks, makes him wait forever for a hearing, and then when he gets one, has the right to sentence him to more time to pay for something he never meant to have happen. No way you can convince me this system is fair."

Then I stood up, threw my napkin down, and announced that I was too full for dessert. Normally Dad would say something about my asking to be excused, but he obviously could tell I was upset, and he let me leave without saying anything. Mom didn't even remind me to take my plate to the sink.

A little later, when I was just sitting down at my desk to start some work, Dad came in my room.

"If you should feel like talking, Jeb, I'll be in my study."

"I *don't* feel like talking," I said, but it came out with a blast, like my anger was automatically loaded and just waiting to go off.

"I didn't say you did, Jeb. I said if you *should* feel like talking, I'm here."

My father the grammarian, I thought. Then I just blurted out, "It figures you'd make an issue over words. Lawyers love to deal with words, instead of doing real things like . . . like . . ."

"Like setting Noel free?" Dad completed my thought. "I can't do that, Jeb. It's not within my power to do that."

When I looked up at him, Dad was standing by the door, already halfway out. I got a tremendously guilty twinge that what I'd said, or the way I said it, had widened the space between us. I don't know what or why, but something made me strike out again at him.

"You don't give a damn what happens to Noel. If you did, you'd get him out of that hole and bring him home. If that S.O.B. Coopersmith had his way, any kid that cops chewing gum in the supermarket would get life."

I hadn't planned to say it. I'd even made a pact with myself to keep my anger about this inside. But here it was, the words spinning out faster than I could keep them in.

Dad walked back into the room. As he came closer, for

one crazy flash of a moment I thought he was going to hit me, but he only asked, "May I sit down, son?"

Before I even had a chance to answer, he sat down on the edge of my bed. I suddenly saw this big, formal man was tired, really beat, like what he wanted or needed most of all was just to rest. The hair on top of his head looked thinner than I remembered. For the first time it seemed like my father was losing his jaunty, sporting look. He looked older. Someday, I was thinking, he'll be an old man.

"Let me explain something to you, Jeb, because I don't think you've got this straight," he said.

I felt myself wince inside at how condescending he sounded, but when I looked up and saw how sad and tired he seemed, I couldn't be angry.

"I may be a lawyer, Jeb, but that doesn't mean I can control the law. Nor does it mean that I'm above the law, or that my children are."

"But you don't seem to even care if Noel gets put away," I blurted out.

"Of course I care," Dad said. "I care very deeply. I care very, very much what happens to Noel."

"But you don't look like it. You look like you couldn't care less." I was screaming in spite of myself now.

"Maybe I don't show the way I feel the way another person might, Jeb, but I care very much what happens to my son, and I want to help him as much as you do." Dad was looking straight at me now, right into my eyes, and it was hard not to turn away. "I care about you too, Jeb."

Now my father's words were coming slower. He sounded lots less sure of himself than he had on the subject of the law, lots less in control. As though he had to be very careful, as though maybe he shouldn't say it at all.

"Something makes me feel that what's happening to Noel almost could have happened to you. Your being so close and all. I don't know. It's just a feeling, I guess. An intuition. Sometimes what happens is a matter of timing, being at the wrong place at the wrong time. And sometimes it's even a matter of chance. What happened to Noel at the blockhouse was one nightmare of a bad break."

I could hardly believe I was hearing my father say these things.

"Do you really mean that, Dad? Do you really mean you think Noel had a bad break and doesn't deserve to be punished the way he is?"

Dad thought for a moment, looked down at the floor, and then said, "There are two parts to my answer, Jeb. Yes, I believe Noel was unlucky. But no, I didn't say he shouldn't be punished. Those are two very different things."

I felt like I'd been tricked into hoping too hard for something I couldn't have after all.

"You may not like it," Dad was saying, "but the legal system we have says that when an individual has broken the law, he must pay for what he's done."

"But he never meant to do it!" My voice was too high, too whiny, like a little kid complaining at not having his way. Like Pete sounded the other day. "What happened was nothing Noel intended to have happen. It was an accident that the blockhouse collapsed and all the flooding and damage happened."

"But Noel caused it to happen," Dad said, "and a per-

114

son is held legally responsible for the consequences of his acts, intentional or not."

The word "consequences" took me right back to the Robinson horse-pasture prank. I knew that my father was right, that what he was saying was the truth: a truth based on legal fact, not opinion. It was something you just couldn't argue about. When I looked up, I saw something I'd never seen before: there were tears in my father's eyes. It made me want to cry.

"I'm sorry for what I said before," I told Dad. "I mean about your not caring what happens to Noel. I'm sorry I said what I did."

15

It's Sunday night, and I have a French test, a calculus quiz, and a lab report in chemistry all due tomorrow. And guess what? I haven't done anything.

I also have a book review due this week in English, and I haven't read the book, which is Faulkner's *As I Lay Dying*. Actually, I started it, but you wouldn't believe how obscure it is. I mean, just the first few pages made me want to lie down and die myself.

Mr. Manoff, our English teacher, said the book uses this technique called "stream of consciousness," which means that the writer, Faulkner, has his character say whatever comes to mind. Actually, it's a lot like how I'm thinking about things now.

I'm having the worst time concentrating on anything lately. Except Stevie, that is. Last night, Saturday, we had her place to ourselves because her mother was out on a date with this doctor she's been going with.

Stevie says that since her mom's been dating Dr. Wallace, she's been in the most incredibly great mood. She never hassles Stevie anymore about what she does and just takes this really laid-back attitude toward everything. Lately she's been saying things to Stevie like, "I know I can trust you. Just use good judgment, dear."

Last night Mrs. Farr was in the city with Dr. Wallace— he works at New York Hospital and lives in New York somewhere so he can be close to his patients—and Stevie's brother Robby was sleeping over at a friend's house.

It was really neat. Kind of like playing house, in a way. I got there around six o'clock and Stevie and I made dinner together.

It was fun cooking with Stevie. She'd taken some steaks out of the freezer before I got there, and even though it's not summer anymore, it wasn't all that cold out so we decided to cook them on the grill. Steaks always taste better when you cook them over charcoal.

Stevie came up with the idea of making this great potato salad that she learned how to make from her grandmother. You take some eggs and some potatoes—we used those little red ones about the size of golf balls—and boil them up together in the same pot. Then you chop up the eggs when they get hard-boiled, skin the potatoes, cut them up, and mix them and the eggs together with some mayonnaise and a little vinegar and pepper while everything's still warm.

The other thing we were going to have with the steak and potato salad was some garlic bread. But that didn't work out so well. Stevie had a big long loaf of bread—one of those Italian type loaves—which we cut in half the long way. Then we smeared lots of butter real thick on both halves and sprinkled garlic powder over that. We put the bread on the high rack of the oven and turned it on "broil." Then we went outside to watch the steaks and forgot about the bread, which we put on much too early anyway.

Suddenly we smelled something burning, and sure enough, by the time we got there, the garlic bread was all charred and black and the oven was smoking and the whole house smelled of burning garlic.

We turned on the fan over the stove to let out the smoke and get rid of the smell, but it hardly did a thing, so Stevie got a can of Lysol spray, and we sprayed the whole kitchen. I mean the *whole* kitchen. We took turns, and then at one point, after the can was practically empty, Stevie even started spraying the stuff at me. I grabbed the can from her and tried to spray her back, but she started this fake screaming routine.

"If you don't stop this minute, Jeb Gray, I'll start hollering loud enough for the neighbors to hear that there's a man in my house who's attacking me."

We both got hysterical laughing, but then we got serious again about dinner. Stevie notice that the garlic butter from the bread had dripped down on the bottom of the oven since we didn't remember to put foil paper under the bread. So we had to get out some oven cleaner and take care of that too, and by the time we were finished with the oven, we'd practically let the steaks burn.

But all things considered, the dinner worked out really well and tasted great. I never knew how much timing and coordination go into getting a whole meal cooked and ready at the same time.

We decided to eat outside at the picnic table, and then when we were done we brought all the dishes and the other stuff inside to wash up. But before we ever got to washing them, we got a little distracted.

I guess it kind of hit us both at the same time. I mean being alone in a house by ourselves and the sun going down outside and the house being warm and dark inside and all. We were really caught by some pretty heavy feelings that were happening for both of us.

We were standing in the kitchen, and I just put my arms around Stevie from behind at one point and she swung around and then we were holding each other and kissing each other harder and harder and everything was going kind of crazy now and it felt like time had either stopped dead still or was speeding up faster and faster out of control.

We wound up going up to Stevie's room, where we've never really spent much time before—I mean alone like that with no one home. Her mother's always been in the house somewhere or we were just getting something we needed and leaving right away. That kind of thing.

But this was different. Right away we were on her bed and really getting carried away and it was all going so fast now that the details are kind of a blur.

I know I had Stevie's shirt off and her bra open, and Stevie had her hand on my jeans where I'd gotten so hard

119

it felt like I was going to explode the minute she touched me.

I started fumbling for my belt and saying something to Stevie about wanting her now and that the time was right, and I'm not sure if she was saying anything but she wasn't stopping me either, and before I knew it we were there with me on top of her and both of us had our jeans open and pulled down.

That was when Stevie said something that's the only thing I remember up to that point. She sounded really scared, and almost like she was going to cry, which was why I was able to stop myself so fast. I guess the way she sounded made me scared too.

"Jeb, we can't," she was saying, right in my ear. "We can't now. It's not right. It's not like how we've promised each other we wanted it to be."

And even though I never wanted a girl like that before, I knew Stevie was right and that having each other that way would be wrong for us. Not wrong in some moral-minded way, like sex is wrong before you're married or anything like that. But wrong because of the timing. I mean, with Stevie it's always been a special kind of thing. Not just kicks or sex, like with some girls I've known, but something special and deeper than that. And if Stevie and I are going to really have an affair some time, we've both said it's something we want to agree on together and kind of plan out. Not just get carried away on the spur of the moment.

We were still holding each other, and I was really hot and not under control yet. I guess Stevie sensed that what I was going through holding back and all was more than

I could deal with, because she asked me in this very sweet and shy-sounding voice, "Can I help you, Jeb? Can I?"

I took her hand then and put it on me and held it as I showed her what to do. At first she kind of clutched at my hand as I started to take it away, as though she was scared to be on her own like that. But I told her, "That's right, Stevie. Just like you're doing," and then she kept doing it until I came. Just as I was coming, I guess when she could feel all the wetness, she called out, "Jeb!" in this surprised-sounding way, and then I held her really tight and told her, "I love you, Stevie. I really love you," which was the first time I ever told her like that. I mean, I've written it lots of times in notes and on cards and stuff, and we've sort of talked about it indirectly, but I've never said, "I love you" to her just like that.

And then she said back to me, "I love you too, Jeb. And I know I always will."

"Me too," I told her, and we hugged each other harder.

16

Noel's hearing date comes up this week, and then they decide whether he has to serve more time or whether they set him free.

Dad said that if they do set him free, there'll at least be a fine. What Noel did is called a "crime against society," and in cases like this the court usually rules in favor of some form of paying back society for what has been harmed or destroyed.

I got a quick note from Noel on Monday, the first in a while. All he had to say was:

Jeb, D-Day is Thursday, October 15. Keep your fingers crossed for me. Noel.

P.S. In case you couldn't figure it out, "D" is for the big Decision.

I told Stevie about the note, and we both thought it would be nice to get a group together on Saturday *if* they let Noel out. Stevie even asked her mother if we could use their house, and her mom said that'd be OK, *if* we have no more than a dozen kids.

Everyone liked the idea a lot when Stevie and I started passing around the word about the party for Noel. Some of the guys—I think it was Steve Sellers and Joey Wilson—started calling it a victory party, and the name kind of stuck. I thought that was going a bit too far; I mean, after all, whatever happens from here on out, you can't exactly call Noel's situation a success story. But the good part is that the kids seem like they want to rally around Noel and give him a real big welcome back, and I think that'll be nice for him after all the time he's spent out of circulation and all.

When I was getting my books together at my locker at the end of school today, Rich Winkler came over and said he'd heard there was going to be a victory party for Noel on Saturday night and could he come too.

"I think what they're doing to Noel sucks, Jeb," Rich told me. "I really think they handed him a raw deal, sticking him in the clink with a bunch of assholes."

You've got to admit Rich has a real way with words. I don't think that guy can get one sentence out without at least a couple of obscenities in it. But Rich is a good kid, and he obviously really cares about Noel.

Even though Stevie and I had rounded up at least a

dozen kids for the party by then, I kind of felt badly saying no to Rich, so I told him, "Sure you can come. We want all Noel's friends who care about him, but come by yourself because Mrs. Farr doesn't want the party to get too big, and we already have close to the limit."

"Greato," Rich said. "Let me know what I can do to help."

That was Wednesday. Thursday was the day of Noel's hearing. It didn't go exactly as we expected or hoped it would. Noel got sentenced to finish out this semester in a boys' training school. It's not exactly jail, but it's hardly freedom either. He's going to earn credit for his semester after all, so if he passes everything he won't have to repeat, and at the same time he'll have to be doing some kind of community service to make up for the damage that he caused.

Judge Coopersmith let him out on bail. Noel has to be transferred from Culver Juvenile Detention Center to Gregoria, the school for boys where he has to serve his time, so they gave him the weekend to spend at home. But because the hearing was only on Thursday, Coopersmith was such a stickler that he said Noel had to wait until Friday to leave Culver for the weekend. I just couldn't believe that part. What a feelingless bastard that guy must be.

It's all really hard to believe. I mean, while he was in Culver it was easy to tell myself, Well, they made a mistake about Noel, and when they really look at who he is and what happened, they'll let him off. But that's not what happened.

Mom and Dad attended the hearing, and when they

came home and told me and Pete about the outcome, they looked like they'd been through a war. When Dad came to the part about bail and Noel having to wait the extra day until the weekend to come home, he looked almost like he was going to cry, and then he said sadly to Mom, "I guess Coopersmith's tougher than I thought, Laura."

As soon as they finished telling us, Mom and Dad went upstairs to their room, and they didn't come out again until dinner around six, when all Mom made was some soup and sandwiches. No one said a word as we sat around eating in the kitchen. It was like someone had died, it was so depressing.

Whenever bad things have happened in the past, Mom's usually the one who tries to hang in there and look on the bright side of things, but this time she seemed completely blown away. She didn't have a cheery thought or a hopeful word to offer anyone. And even though I wanted to say something to make it easier for her, I couldn't think of a thing that would help.

It was even more depressing what happened after the news got passed around at school and all the kids found out about Noel's being sent to Gregoria. By Friday we were telling everyone who was coming to the victory party that it wouldn't be a victory party, but that we were having a party anyway, just to show our support for Noel. He only has these few days before being sent to Gregoria, so we figure while he's out on bail the guy deserves a show of friendship.

All of a sudden by Friday afternoon when Stevie and I were firming up plans for the party, everyone seemed to have lost interest in coming.

I ran into Rich Winkler in chemistry lab at the end of Friday, and when I said, "See you around seven tomorrow night at Stevie's, Rich," he wasn't so sure.

"I don't know, Jeb. There's lots of stuff I'd rather do with my Saturday night than hear jail stories."

I got really mad when he said that. "You sure changed your tune fast, Rich."

"Oh, come on, Jeb," he said, "Noel's getting what he deserves. Face it, man."

Two of Stevie's friends, Margo and Alyn, who had said they'd be at the party, called Stevie Friday night to say they didn't think their parents would be too happy about their going to a party for Noel after what happened and all.

Ace Clayton, who played on Noel's baseball team last spring, said he'd come when I met him in the parking lot after school on Thursday, but after the word about the hearing got out and I saw him again at school on Friday, he said, "I figured he'd have to serve some more time for the mess he made!"

"Hey, come on, Ace, that's no way to talk about a friend," I told him, and then I asked, kind of nervously by now, "We gonna see you tomorrow night at Stevie's?"

"Something's come up, Jeb," Ace told me, "and I don't think I can get free after all."

I just walked away when he said that. There was nothing left to say.

John Clugston and Dick Miller were kind of noncommittal. You get the feeling everyone's suddenly turned traitor or is just hanging back waiting to hear what the other guys are going to decide. Stevie says Jill Johnson and some of the other girls we talked to are not sure about coming anymore either.

It really pisses me off that all these people who've known Noel for years are suddenly not hanging in there for him. There's no way I'm not going to have some sort of party to welcome him home. The guy's been away for six weeks. I don't care what some judge did to him in court; I'm going to stand by him and the hell with everyone else.

Well, Stevie said at least Jenny, who's her best friend, is coming, and Ellen Morley said she'd be there—Noel took her out a couple of times last summer—and maybe we can get a few more people together before Saturday night.

——17——

Dad went to get Noel at Culver after he came home from work on Friday. Mom seemed real nervous and jittery while we were waiting for them to get back. She fixed a nice dinner with all Noel's favorite foods: lasagna, salad with Russian dressing, apple pie for dessert. Ever since I can remember, Noel's loved apple pie, and whenever there's a special occasion, like his birthday or his graduation from junior high, Mom makes him an apple pie. It's kind of funny to see birthday candles stuck in the crust of an apple pie, but that's what Noel always asked for, and that's what he got.

The moment Noel and Dad walked in, I knew the dinner was going to be a disaster. Dad looked tense and angry, like he and Noel had had an argument or something, and Noel looked awful. He must've lost ten pounds while he was away, and his skin was all pale and white, like he hadn't seen the sun for months. His hair was all greasy-looking, and the minute he walked in he told Mom he wasn't hungry and headed up to his room. Dad mumbled something to Mom about leaving "the boy" alone, so Mom just went about serving dinner to me, Pete, and Dad like nothing unusual was happening. As Noel was leaving the kitchen to go upstairs, he stopped for a moment when he saw Pete and kind of tousled his hair. All through dinner, whenever I looked over at Pete, I'd see him slowly rubbing his hand through the same spot on his hair that Noel had rubbed.

The most depressing part of the meal was that Mom decided to leave Noel's place set—probably just in case he changed his mind and came back down. The only things that got said the whole meal were things like "Pass the butter." Mom didn't serve the apple pie, and when every-one was finished eating, while Pete was clearing his place, he went over to where Noel's place was set and kind of whispered to the empty chair, "Come on, Maypo, you don't have to save his place anymore. He's not coming and dinner's done now." Mom looked over at Dad when Pete said that, and it was really sad to see the look they gave each other. Almost desperate, like they didn't know how to handle any of this anymore.

Later, after dinner, I went upstairs and knocked on Noel's door. When I went in, he was lying on his back on his bed listening to his rock tapes. Noel has this incredible collection of tapes. He's got practically all of the Rolling

Stones, Led Zeppelin, and The Police. With some of the money we made last summer cutting grass, he bought himself this really neat Aiwa box, which he used to take along when we went places.

"Hey, Noel," I said, "remember how Doc Coulter used to go bats when we'd play your box too loud over at his place?"

I was looking for a way to open things up, but Noel obviously wasn't in the mood. All he said was, "Yeah, the bastard."

I decided to change the subject, so I told him Stevie and I were having a get-together for him over at her place tomorrow night. I was afraid he'd say he didn't want to go, but all he said, which in a way was worse because it seemed so weird, was, "That's nice."

The party was a real bummer. I mean, with just Stevie, Jenny, Ellen, me, and Noel, it was kind of hard sitting around pretending we were having a normal ordinary party. And no one else showed up.

Noel was real quiet and uncommunicative the whole time, which made it even harder. There we were sitting in Stevie's family room with bowls of potato chips and pretzels like we were expecting a whole army of people, and no one was eating or talking very much.

Dancing was out because with only five of us it seemed kind of a dumb thing to do, so we just wound up playing some of Noel's tapes, which I asked him to bring along.

After a while I took Stevie inside to the kitchen and told her I thought Noel was really depressed and that maybe he and I should just take off somewhere and be by ourselves for a while. Stevie thought that was a good idea, so I went back inside and said to Noel, "Hey, how about the two of us going for a walk and getting some air?"

Noel said that'd be fine, but he seemed indifferent about the idea, as though anything I might've suggested would've been OK. A crazy thought passed through my mind for a second. I imagined saying to him, Hey, Noel, how about we go jump off the Brooklyn Bridge? and I imagined that he'd just say OK.

It was strange seeing Noel act that way, so subdued and almost agreeable. Usually Noel's got a real strong will, and if I come up with some plan, he usually comes up with something else he'd rather do.

I was really uncomfortable being with him in that mood. I mean, I like being agreed with and getting my way and all, but I guess I was counting on being with Noel the way I knew him, not this other way. It didn't feel like I was with someone I knew at all. It was more like being with a stranger.

Something really disconcerting happened when we were leaving. Stevie had to remind Noel to take his box, the Aiwa he bought last summer, and all the tapes he'd brought along. When Stevie reminded him, all he said was, "Oh, that's right. I guess I should take my stuff if I'm leaving."

He almost sounded dazed, and Stevie and I kind of looked at each other uneasily.

"You want to walk back to our place," I asked Noel as we left, "so we can drop your box and those tapes off?"

"Nah, I don't think so," he said.

"Don't you think it'll get a little heavy carrying around

that load of stuff?" I asked, hoping he'd change his mind.

"Yeah, OK," was all he said, so I started heading toward our house. I got that funny feeling again of not recognizing Noel.

When we got home, I was glad that the folks were already upstairs in their room. I could see their window lighted up behind the shade, so I knew they were watching TV or something. It was ten o'clock on my watch, and I saw that Pete's window was dark, so I figured he'd already hit the sack for the night.

Noel and I went around to the back door and came in through the kitchen. Noel just sort of stood there by the door like he was a guest or something, so I went over and took the box and tapes from him and set them down on the counter. I guess I was feeling kind of like he *was* a guest and I was the host, so I asked him if he was thirsty and wanted a Coke. He nodded and took the can I handed him in the same way he was taking whatever suggestions anyone made, like it didn't matter one way or the other to him what he did or didn't do. And then he just left the Coke on the table instead of drinking it.

We were sitting there in the kitchen, at the breakfast table, and I had this feeling that I had to say something soon or we'd get stuck and wouldn't ever be able to start talking. I just sort of blurted out the first thing that came to mind.

"How'd you feel about the decision?" I asked.

The minute the words came out, the question sounded ridiculously dumb to me, and I wished I could take it back.

When Noel didn't answer—he just sort of shrugged

instead—I said, "Coopersmith sure handed you a raw deal."

There was a real long silence then, which I finally broke.

"Hey, thanks for your letters from Culver. I guess they gave you a pretty rough time in there."

"Not as bad for me as for some of the others," Noel said. "One guy—his name was Demo, only fourteen years old—they gave this kid a week of solitary confinement for telling a guard that he wished some guy were dead."

I couldn't believe it. "A week of solitary for wishing, just *wishing*, someone were dead? Not even helping it along?"

"Nope. Just wishing," Noel said. "I guess Demo figured, What the hell, if a guy can't wish, he may as well be dead himself. Before the week was up, some guard with a meal tray found the kid hanging by a sheet in his cell."

I was speechless when Noel told me that. The only thing I finally thought of to say was, "Fourteen years old. Jeez. . . ."

Suddenly Noel sat up straighter and looked a little more with it and started talking with a lot more feeling.

"You know what Pete did?" he asked me. "He broke that baseball bank he's had for years—the one he keeps on his dresser that looks like a real baseball—and told Mom before she left for my hearing that he wanted her to use what was in it for me. He did it because he found out from someone that the judge might fine me instead of sentencing me to more time." Then he said, much more quietly, "I guess he was hoping."

I told Noel, "I think *I* said something like that to Pete

once when he was worried about what they could do to you."

"Did you tell the little guy they could put me away some more?" Noel's voice was angry and bitter, and I could see tears in his eyes.

"Yeah, I told him that might happen, but I don't think I really believed it'd come to that."

I reached out to put my hand on Noel's arm, but before I could touch him, he pulled away and kind of hugged both his arms around himself. I had to stop talking. I was too choked up with tears of my own now.

After a while Noel said, "Yeah, well, it doesn't matter. It was bound to happen."

"What was bound to happen?" I asked him.

He stood up from where he was sitting and said, "Something horrible like this. Some people have unlucky stars, Jeb, that's all."

"Hey." I wanted to argue with him, to encourage him somehow. I felt desperate to find the right thing to say, but nothing came to me, and before I could say much of anything, Noel was looking like he was getting set to leave.

"Think I'll go take a walk by myself for a while, Jeb."

"Hey, it's early still," I told him. "You wanna go for some pizza or ice cream? How about we go over to Lumpy's or something?"

"Nah, I don't think so," Noel said.

I saw his Aiwa and the tapes sitting over on the kitchen counter, and I asked him if he wanted me to put them up in his room.

"Listen, Jeb, why don't you just keep those things?"

"You mean your Aiwa and all those tapes?" I was so

startled by what he said that I couldn't believe I'd heard right. But I couldn't seriously just take and keep Noel's box and tapes like that, so I said, "Well, you'll be out soon, so sure, if you like, I'll keep this stuff safe while you're away, and then you'll have them back when you get out."

"Thanks, Jeb. You do that."

He slapped me on the shoulder, and I felt like I was going to bawl my head off if I said anything then. All I managed, as he went out the back door, was, "See ya later, kid," and then he was gone.

As Noel turned his back to leave, I saw—or, rather, I noticed for the first time all night—that the shirt he was wearing was the blue baseball shirt with *Wakefield Wonders* on the front and GRAY in big white letters across the back.

18

What I have to say is so impossible that I almost can't bring myself to say it. But I've got to. Just to say it so it's out and said.

Noel killed himself last night. Shot himself through the head with an old hunting pistol he got hold of God knows where.

Grady Markham, whose house is just down the road from where Robinson's was before it washed out, heard a single gunshot from somewhere up near the reservoir around midnight last night, and when the police investigated, they found Noel lying dead about a hundred feet from the blockhouse. The pistol was next to his body: suicide.

I didn't find out until this morning, when Mom woke me at eight o'clock. She and Dad found out last night, and even though Dad had to go out in the middle of the night to identify Noel, I slept through it all. And so must've Pete.

I was sleeping when Mom came in to tell me, one of those really deep dream sleeps that's so hard to wake up from. But the moment I saw her I was wide awake. Mom's face was like a ghost of Mom more than Mom herself. I think overnight she turned into an old woman. Her cheeks looked sunken in, and her eyes were red and swollen and ringed all around with deep black shadows. I knew in that very first instant that she'd never ever be the same again.

It took a while for me to feel anything when Mom first told me. I mean, the facts sunk in right away. And somehow, I don't know how, they even made sense. Noel was so depressed last night, the way he was acting. And then his leaving the house alone, all by himself. All that stuff came back to me right away, but it was like something else was waiting somewhere behind the scenes to happen in my mind. Some connection that was waiting to get made.

And then it happened. It hit me like a falling beam. *I should have stopped him*. I should've seen what was happening and known what Noel was going to do. I should've stayed with him. Or made him stay with me. I could've saved him if I had.

That was when the feelings hit me. Up until then it was just facts. And then it was like a flood of feelings coursing through me like, like . . . like water bursting through a floodgate.

Then suddenly I was all in motion. Pulling on my clothes, my running shoes. Mom kept asking, "What are you doing, Jeb? Where are you going?" But I couldn't even give her an answer. I didn't know what I was doing. I had no idea where I was going. I just had to keep moving.

I think I called out, "I have to go," or something like that as I ran out of the house. I didn't think I knew where I was going, but part of me knew where I wanted to go, because my legs kept pumping and I just kept running until I wound up at the hillside where the blockhouse is.

I don't know how I climbed the hill in the state I was in. It's very steep and rocky, and I never even slowed down. I must've kept tripping and falling and pulling myself up again and again, because my pants got all torn up at the knees and my hands were rough and scraped and bleeding. I didn't notice them right away, but when I got up to the blockhouse and started looking around and really registering what had happened, I began to cry, I mean really sob, and when I covered my face with my hands, I saw the blood on them, all caked with dirt from the hillside.

It sounds really sicko what I did when I got up there, but something made me want to find the spot where Noel killed himself. I had a tremendous need to find the exact spot where he died, kind of like if I could find where he died, I might somehow be able to trace backward to where, or when, he was living. It doesn't make sense exactly, I know, but it was this very powerful instinct.

I never really found the exact spot where Noel died because someone—the police or the rescue workers—had raked the ground or thrown shovelfuls of fresh dirt where

Noel's body must have lain. I guess I was looking for blood and traces of him, but there was nothing, just a neat little clearing in the rubble and overgrowth of the hillside, about a hundred feet from the blockhouse.

When I realized that this was it, or all that was left of it—whatever *it* was exactly—the first thing I felt was anger. Like how the hell could they have done this, cleaned up and made disappear the last traces of Noel's life?

I guess I kind of lost my mind with grief. I was crying so hard and calling out things like, "Bring him back, please, please bring Noel back." And then I was right there, down on the ground, in the cleaned-up little clearing that was all that was left of Noel's life and death. I must have lain there like that, sobbing, screaming, and pounding on the ground, until I'd worked myself up into such an hysterical pitch that I think I finally blacked out or fainted from exhaustion.

It was sometime toward noon that someone very gently rolled me over onto my back. I felt a hand on each shoulder, and I remember actually being aware of the evenness of the pressure on each one.

When I opened my eyes and looked up, I was blinded by the sun. The next thing I remember was a familiar voice saying, "It's time to come home now," and then again, "It's time to come home now, son."

By then my eyes were getting accustomed to the light, and my father's face—filled with pain—blurred into view.

"Snuffed out like a candle," the minister said at Noel's funeral. Snuffed out. What a stupid, feeble description. The minister didn't even know him. He had no idea, and neither did any of the rest of them, of what Noel was really all about. The minister talked endlessly about what a "bright and beautiful light" Noel was, and how his memory will always shine on in our hearts like an eternal flame. What an idiot. He mixed up all his metaphors—you can't be snuffed out like a candle *and* be like an eternal flame. And everyone all around me sniffling and crying into handkerchiefs. I felt like standing up in the middle of the stupid service and screaming at him to shut up.

None of them ever saw Noel's true brightness, or what was brave and good in him. Except little Pete. Pete was white and stiff at the funeral. Didn't cry and barely moved. Just walked like a little soldier from the church to the car. At the cemetery, when they lowered the coffin down into the ground, he flinched and looked away, and that was all. No tears, nothing. Noel's life wasn't snuffed out. It was smothered and destroyed.

It's been a week since the funeral, but it could just as well be a day or a year. I can't tell one day from another, or the days from the nights. It all just blurs together.

Except when I think of Noel and how he died, and then I can feel myself losing control and coming apart inside. I keep imagining I'm hearing a gunshot—every bang or loud noise around me—and whenever I do, it feels like my mind is shattering. I hear the sound. And then I feel the cold, the ice-cold fear everywhere. And it happens again and again inside me.

I try to hang on, to grab hold of something to anchor myself to reasons and meanings. But I can't find any. I try to think of Stevie, but that makes it worse. It makes me feel that because something as good as Stevie was happening in my life, I had to pay a price; the price I paid for Stevie was Noel, or something like that. Or maybe what I feel is that the price I paid is a clear conscience, which I know I'll never have again.

I've tried to think of college, of the future that everyone is always promising will be so bright and beautiful. But nothing seems real anymore but Noel's death and how he died. I just can't believe, or bring myself to believe, that a future is going to happen and Noel won't be there.

I always hate it when people say—and they say it all the time—"Youth is wasted on the young." There's so much I remember, so much I can still see and feel from when I was young. So many memories that are filled up with Noel. I think I felt more then than now, more than I ever will again. Except for the pain, which just grows and grows.

Maybe it's because everything was once so simple and clear, and now nothing's clear or simple anymore. The feeling of my mind shattering wipes it all away. The dizziness, the spinning, the craziness that takes hold of me. The terror. And the question that never stops because there is no answer. Why did Noel have to die; and why, for what reason, was I the one to survive?

19

I got accepted to Yale yesterday, Thursday, December eighteenth. That's when the letter arrived. It was waiting for me when I came home. I couldn't help thinking how ironic it was that the letter telling me I was going to Yale next year arrived only two months—nine weeks to the day—after Noel got told he was going to Gregoria.

It isn't that going to Yale feels like going to jail—no rhyme intended. It was just like my fate was suddenly sealed. There it was: the shape and form of my future suddenly falling into place.

Mom was in the house when I got home, but she was obviously being real discreet so I'd have privacy while I read the letter. She was off in her weaving room, and she just left the letter on the kitchen table where I couldn't miss it.

When I read the letter I felt absolutely nothing. Not happy or relieved or even surprised. I guess I was kind of expecting to get in. I mean, the teachers and Mrs. Galsworthy, the college advisor, were all real encouraging, so I knew I had a pretty good chance. But when it actually happened, it didn't matter anymore.

I knew Mom was waiting to hear what the letter said, so on my way to my room I stopped in her studio. I didn't mean to put a damper on the whole thing, but all I could bring myself to do was to tell her I was accepted and drop the letter on her loom and then walk out. I just wasn't in the mood to make a whole big production out of it.

I went to my room and just lay on my back on my bed, looking at the ceiling. I had tons of work to do, but I couldn't even unload my knapsack. I just lay there looking at the ceiling and feeling horrible about everything. Especially horrible about not feeling wonderful about getting into Yale.

It must've been about half an hour later when Mom came in. She stuck her head in my half-opened doorway and said, "You working, Jeb?"

"Just thinking, not working," I told her, and then I got up from the bed and went over to my desk and sat down. I have this swivel chair, and I turned it around to face her as she came into my room.

"Are you pleased about the letter from Yale? I'm very proud of you, you know."

I felt crummy when I said what I said then, but it just came out. "Come on, Mom. Since when do you go in for all that Ivy League snob appeal? Maybe Dad does, but you've never been impressed by big names and fancy labels."

Mom didn't say anything at first. She just crossed the room and sat down on my bed. I watched her kick off her scuffy house slippers—the pale blue ones she always wears with the pompom things on the end of them—and tuck her legs up under her Indian-style the way she does when she's sitting down to have a talk.

Suddenly she looked really young again, not old and haggard like she's looked since Noel died. It went through my mind that she was once a college kid—once long ago before she had kids of her own, before she lost her own kid. And I remembered she never went to a place like Yale or even got to go away to school at all, the way I'd be doing. Mom went to Hunter College in New York City where she was raised, and she lived at home with her parents. The first time she ever lived away from home was when she married Dad and moved into his bachelor apartment on Morningside Heights, while he was finishing his last year of Columbia Law School. It feels strange as you get older to see your parents' lives begin to fall in place and make sense in ways you never thought about when you were younger.

Then Mom started talking. Her voice was soft but very serious.

"Yale is more than a name or a label, Jeb. It's something you've worked toward for a very long time. A place you've *earned* going to by hard work and good grades." She poked my knapsack full of books with her toe. "A *lot* of hard work, Jeb. You deserve to go to Yale."

I was spinning slowly around on my swivel chair as she talked. Each time I faced my desk, away from Mom, I gave my bottom drawer by the kneehole a kick, just enough to take out the bad feelings that were gnawing at me.

"I thought the Yale letter would make you happier than you seem," Mom said.

Her voice sounded coaxing, and I felt sorry she knew I wasn't particularly happy about getting into Yale.

"I *am* glad about getting in," I told her. "It's just not that big a deal, I guess. I mean lots of kids applied Early Action and are getting letters."

"But none of them have been through what you've been through, since . . . since Noel . . ."

She couldn't say the rest, the part about Noel killing himself, but the suddenness of her bringing him up in that way, at that time, took me by surprise. I wasn't expecting that part of my territory to be invaded. I don't talk to Mom about Noel. Talking can't make what happened not have happened, so there's no use talking. It only makes it worse.

"I almost get the feeling you blame yourself, Jeb," Mom said. "It's not your fault what happened. You were always the very best brother to Noel."

"That's a lie," I told her. "I knew Noel was going to open up some water valves at the blockhouse before he did it. I should've stopped him, persuaded him not to."

"Sometimes a person can't be persuaded," Mom said, and her voice was small and high, now, and very far away.

"Noel didn't deserve what they did to him," I told her angrily.

"*Nobody* deserves what happened to Noel."

"It's not fair," I said. "It's not fair that he'll never have a future. . . ."

"No, it's not fair, my darling, not fair at all," Mom said, and then she held her head in her hands and sobbed like her heart and soul were shattered in a million bits and pieces that could never ever get put back together again.

20

I was invited to Stevie's house for Sunday dinner today. They didn't come right out and say the meal was meant to celebrate my getting into Yale, but I could tell they were making it special for that reason. Usually the Farrs just have a casual meal for lunch and then sometimes they go out for pizza or Chinese food for dinner, but this was a big Sunday middle-of-the-afternoon type meal.

They had turkey with stuffing—this really delicious stuffing with chestnuts and raisins in it that Stevie said was her Mom's own recipe—and for dessert they served a chocolate cake. Stevie and her brother Robby and her mother were all smiling and giggling when Stevie brought the cake out, and then when she put it down on the table, I saw a big blue "Y" for Yale squiggled in the middle of the cake.

I felt kind of embarrassed at first when I saw it, and I just blurted out, "Hey, you didn't have to do all that."

"You mean putting a 'Y' on the cake?" Stevie said.

"Yeah," I said. "The big blue 'Y' for Yale."

Stevie had this twinkling little look on her face that means something funny's coming. "Oh, that. It doesn't stand for Yale, you boob, it stands for 'yesterday.' I put it on the cake so I'd remember when I made it."

Robby really howled, and then Stevie and her mother started laughing. I felt real embarrassed at first, and then I had to laugh too. It was really pretty funny.

Afterward, when we were by ourselves, Stevie gave me a little china bulldog. The Yale mascot is a bulldog, and Stevie said the gift was for my getting accepted. It was really sweet, and for the first time since the letter came, it made me feel good about getting in. I could tell Stevie was really proud of me, which I guess made me feel kind of proud of myself too.

Before we went outside, Stevie offered to help her mom clean up, but Mrs. Farr said she'd take care of the dishes and for us to go off and do what we'd like. As we left the kitchen I told Mrs. Farr, "Thanks for the super supper. And for the delicious cake. It was great."

"You're very welcome, Jeb," she said. "We all think it's great about your getting into Yale. I know you'll have a wonderful time up there."

"Thanks again," I told her, and then Stevie and I went outside to the patio where we could see the sun already beginning to set.

It was only around four, but the days are getting shorter now. We sat outside on the brick wall that runs all around the Farrs' patio just watching the sky turn colors from reddish blue to black as the sun went down. The temperature was going down too, and suddenly we both felt really cold. I didn't feel comfortable getting too close to Stevie with Mrs. Farr around, but we did move over toward each other, and it felt nice to feel her sitting right up against me.

The dark blue sweater Stevie was wearing looked black, and the collar and cuffs of her pale blue shirt looked lavender in the evening light. As I watched her profile, I felt like I could actually feel with my eyes the softness of her skin, as though from the times when we'd touched I'd actually memorized the physical feeling and could call it back at will.

"Whatcha thinkin'?" Stevie asked me. For some reason I can't explain, I was thinking about that day with Noel and Pete. I told Stevie about it.

"I was thinking about cicadas and this one time with Noel and Pete when we saw a killer wasp attack one and carry it off."

I began to get this incredibly sad, heavy feeling as I told the last part.

"The cicada never had a chance. The moment it was stung, it was paralyzed, and the wasp just flew away with it to bury it in a cell beneath the ground."

"Like when they put Noel away," Stevie said. "That's when it really ended, when they put him away. He was numb from then on, like he'd been paralyzed by some poison that got in his system."

I was almost crying. "Yeah, he didn't even make it to his seventeenth birthday."

"Jeb . . ."

Stevie reached out her hand toward mine, but I pulled it away and up to my face.

"I know how you miss him, Jeb," she said.

"I always will," I told her, and then I buried my face in both my hands and cried.

The sky had gone completely black now, and the only sound was my sobbing. I could feel Stevie's hand rubbing circles on my back.

After a while, when I stopped crying, Stevie took my hand and kind of wiped it dry with her sleeve. Then she tucked my hand in the pocket of her sweater and held it. I felt some funny-shaped object in there, and when I pulled it out I saw that it was one of those tubes of stuff you use for decorating cakes. The tube was white with a blue heart on it, and then I remembered the chocolate cake and the big blue "Y" on the icing. Stevie smiled.

"Boy, did you ever look surprised when that cake came out with a 'Y' on it!"

"And boy, was that dumb what you said about the 'Y' standing for yesterday," I kidded her.

"But it sure did embarrass you," she teased. "You looked completely thrown off balance."

"Bull!" I told her, and then we both started laughing and jabbing each other in the sides with our elbows and staging a kind of mock wrestling match. Until I fell off the wall.

"See?" Stevie said. "I told you you were thrown off balance. I guess it's true that girls are better balanced than guys, and faster, and prettier, and lighter on our feet, and all the good stuff. . . ."

I started chasing her as she darted back toward the house. Just before she got there, I caught her and put her in a real firm hammerlock. Just enough pressure to hold her, but not enough to hurt her.

"Say Uncle, Stevie, or you're done for," I told her.

"Never," she said, and laughed in my face.

I tightened my hold and told her again. "You'd better give in and say Uncle or else."

"How about Humpty Dumpty, would that do?" she said, and when I laughed, my grip loosened a little and she squirmed free and ran inside.

We landed in the kitchen, laughing and out of breath, just as her Mom was closing the dishwasher.

"The two of you look like you just ran the marathon," Mrs. Farr said.

Just then we heard a car drive up.

"That must be Dr. Wallace," Stevie said.

Stevie's mom went to open the front door. When she was out of hearing range, Stevie whispered to me, "This relationship is getting pretty heavy. He's been coming up here from the city a couple of times a week lately."

"He seems nice enough," I told Stevie.

She nodded like she agreed, but then real fast afterward, like she wasn't so sure after all, she shrugged her shoulders and said, "He's OK, I guess."

"Hey," I said, catching a glimpse of the clock, which said five thirty, "I gotta go. I have a French final tomorrow and a calculus quiz. I'd better call my mother and see if she can come over and get me."

Mrs. Farr and Dr. Wallace were coming in as I said that, and they must've overheard me.

"I can run you home, Jeb," Dr. Wallace said. "My car's right outside."

"Oh, that's all right," I told him. "My mother doesn't mind. She's expecting me to call."

"Come on, Stevie," he said in this really nice, pleasant way. "You and I will drive Jeb home. It'll just take a couple minutes. OK, Joan?"

Mrs. Farr said, "That'll be fine, Sam. How nice of you to offer." And the three of us headed for his car.

When we got to my house I thanked him and said goodbye to Stevie. I'd started walking toward my house when I heard Stevie call, "Oh, Jeb, there's something I almost forgot."

I walked back to the car, where Stevie had rolled down her window to tell me something, and then, before I knew what hit me, she squeezed a whole mess of the blue cake decorating goo in my face.

"We're just having a little celebration," she explained to Dr. Wallace, who looked about as shocked as I felt.

I wiped most of the gunk off with my hand and leaned down to the open window.

"Now I know what the 'Y' really means. It stands for YUCK!"

And I smeared blue goo all over her face. As they were driving off, I heard Stevie laughing and Dr. Wallace saying, "You and your boyfriend make quite a pair, Miss Farr."

21

It's summer again, the end of summer actually, and I leave for freshman orientation next week. Of course it's going to be rough leaving Stevie, but little Pete's the one I'm really worried about. Since Noel died he's changed a lot. I mean, he's still the same basic person he always was, but he's got a big chip on his shoulder these days. Just about anything anyone says or does, Pete reacts kind of defensively. In a way, Pete reminds me more and more of Noel and the way he used to be. Maybe it's his way of making his big brother who died come back to life.

One thing that happened recently that was really sad and said a lot about how much Pete is hurting is something Mom found out from Pete's teacher. Mom was called into school for a conference, and the teacher told her she was concerned about Pete because he was talking about Noel a lot lately in school. Only he wasn't admitting that Noel was dead, just pretending Noel was still here and doing all this stuff that Pete was making up and telling the kids in his class.

Mom tried later to talk to Pete about it, but he got real wild and angry and denied it completely and said his teacher was a jerk and a liar. For almost a wcck after that Pete refused to go to school, just simply would not go, until Dad started taking Pete himself, driving him over instead of his catching the school bus.

Dad's aged a lot this year. He seems slower and just generally older, I guess. He sits by himself sometimes and looks sad and worn down, but when he sees someone coming over, he suddenly gets real busy shuffling papers or turning pages of a magazine, to try to make you think he's the same way he's always been.

I've noticed one good thing that's changed, though, which probably has to do with Dad's feeling sorry about a lot of things that happened between him and Noel. It's almost as though Dad made up his mind to make up for whatever he might've done wrong with Noel by being extra-specially sensitive toward Pete. Like this driving-Pete-to-school thing. Dad would never in a million years have done that before.

I guess I've been thinking a lot lately about how much has changed this year. Including myself. It's been almost a year since Noel raided the blockhouse and went to Culver, which in my mind stands out as the event that marked the beginning of senior year, because right after that we

154

went back to school. Everyone but Noel, that is.

In some ways I think I'm beginning to get some perspective on what happened and on what I've been feeling since Noel died. The sadness never really goes away. I mean, the pain is not as sharp or as strong as it was at the beginning, but the sadness—or maybe "sorrow" is a better word—seems to grow with time, not lessen.

Whenever something happens that Noel would've been part of—should've been part of—I get stopped by the feeling that what's happening has no right to happen without him.

Like track this spring. I'd be out there racing through the countryside feeling free as the breeze, and suddenly I'd think of Noel and how we used to run together through the same places, and I'd feel myself literally slowing down and getting tired, like something had suddenly taken the wind right out of me.

Once or twice I actually stopped running, had to stop, because tears would come and catch in my throat and in my chest till I practically couldn't breathe. I'd stand there sweating and panting, trying to catch my breath, thinking to myself, How can it all be the same? The trees, the sky, the air, the earth? It just didn't make sense that the whole earth was still here but Noel would never walk or run on it again.

I know now what it means to love someone "like a brother." In a way what that means, I think, is that the way a person loves his brother is like the way he loves himself. Of course when Noel was living I never thought that way about him. I mean, a brother was someone you hung around with, someone who was there and who you just took for granted. Not someone you loved and needed in certain ways and without whom you'd never feel the same again.

I think one thing that Noel's death has done is make me a more serious person than I was before. But it's a heavy feeling learning what life is worth by losing a person you love.

Before Noel died, I just took life for granted. The same way I took him and our friendship for granted. You get born, I always figured, you live, and someday when you're old and tired and all used up you die. That's what I thought until Noel died. But when Noel died he wasn't old or tired or used up. He'd hardly even begun to live.

So everything I always thought about the order of life and death got turned inside out and backwards, which made me have to come to terms with the fact that life isn't predictable and no one can really ever count on anything for sure.

Last winter when I got into Yale, I was feeling like my whole future was laid out for me and it didn't matter very much what I thought or felt or even did about it. But I don't feel that way anymore. Now I feel like what matters most is how *I* decide to live, what *I* decide to do, what choices *I* decide to make. I guess what I'm saying is I believe I'm the one who's in charge of making my life go the way I want it to.

Yesterday Mom and I were out gathering apples from the little apple tree we planted a couple of years ago in our yard. This is the first year that it's given any fruit, but because it's still so young and weak, its branches are too frail to stand up under the weight of the apples growing on them. The apples don't know the tree is too young to hold them, so they grow to full size, and then they weigh down the branches, which finally break under the strain.

As we were picking, Mom said, "It reminds me of Noel, this little tree: too young to carry the burden of the fruit it bears."

I asked her, "How long do you think it will take for the tree to be big enough to support the weight of its own fruit?"

"Maybe another four years or so," Mom said.

"Hey," I said, "that's just when I'll be graduating from college."

Mom hesitated for a moment, like she wasn't sure she should say what she was thinking, but then she went ahead.

"Perfect timing. I'll make apple pie to celebrate."

And she hugged me and we laughed.

22

Tomorrow, Sunday, I leave for college. My parents and Pete are driving me up to New Haven in the morning. Stevie and I spent today together, and we just said good-bye, or rather, "So long until the next time," a little while ago. Stevie was in tears, even though we've talked out what my leaving is all about and how it doesn't mean I'm leaving her, just leaving home to go away to school.

But I guess we both know that distance and separation can affect the way people feel about each other, and neither of us wants the distance or time away to make us grow apart.

Stevie packed a picnic lunch, and I picked her up at her house a little after noon. We wanted to go off somewhere in the country where we'd be by ourselves, and I came up with the idea of going up by the Barlow farm. The Barlow farm must be a couple of hundred acres of corn and potatoes, with lots of little dirt roads nearby leading to wooded areas with streams and ponds. It's really beautiful and very private.

When I drove up to Stevie's house and she came out looking all fresh and pretty and eager, I got this tremendous pang about leaving her and leaving home and leaving everything else I've always known. Suddenly it felt like I was going away for good; not just to school, where I'll be coming home for vacations and weekends whenever I want, but like I was leaving forever.

I sat watching Stevie leave her house the way she's done a hundred times when I've come over, seeing her slam the door behind her, turn to double-check that it's closed tight, and then watching the way she has of kind of half skipping, half running to the car. It all suddenly struck me as incredibly special, and I got a mixed-up feeling of having and losing something all at the same time. I was trying to memorize everything, all these tiny details that I usually don't even notice or think about. Kind of like packing to go somewhere and making sure you have every single item that you're going to need. But instead of clothes and toothpaste and real things, I was packing my mind with memories.

Suddenly I saw a bicycle in the rearview mirror coming up fast from behind me. I thought for an instant that it was going to crash right into the rear of my car, and I braced myself. But next thing I knew, I recognized Pete's blond curly head. He was wearing a bathing suit, with a towel hanging like a scarf around his neck, and he was carrying a rolled-up brown bag under one arm. When he reached the car, he skidded to a stop right by my window.

"Hey, Jeb," he said breathlessly, "you forgot this for your picnic. I saw it lying out in the kitchen and thought you'd need it."

I reached for the package and realized he'd brought me the Aiwa cassette player, Noel's box, that I'd left on the kitchen counter, planning to bring it along.

"Hey, thanks," I told Pete. "You even brought me the tapes. Thanks, pal, thanks a lot."

Stevie was in the car next to me now, and Pete leaned into the car.

"Your boyfriend's forgetting stuff today," he told her. "You'd better watch out he doesn't forget how to find his way home later."

"Thanks for the tip, Pete," Stevie told him. "I'll make sure he gets home again, OK? I bet you'll miss Jeb a lot when he's up at school, Pete, and so will I. Maybe you'll come over on your bike sometime and visit me. Would you do that?"

When he didn't say anything, Stevie asked again, "Would you, Pete? I'd really like you to."

"Are you kidding? I'm not gonna miss him," Pete said. "I'll be glad to get rid of him. And anyway, Yale stinks." And he was off down the block, the towel flapping in the wind.

"Wow," Stevie said, "he sounds pretty angry about your going away."

"I never realized *how* angry till just now," I told her, and then, because it was hard to think about Pete's problems without spoiling my mood, I changed the subject and said the weather sure looked great for our picnic.

"Let's go then," Stevie said, and off we went.

We could see Stevie's neighbor Billy Ellsworth and his dad shingling their roof. Stevie waved as we passed Mrs. Ellsworth, who was at the front of their yard picking over a bed of pink flowers.

"I always wonder what big occasion Mrs. Ellsworth is waiting for," Stevie said. "I mean, ever since I've known her, which is practically my whole life, I don't think I've ever seen her once with her hair out of rollers."

As we left her neighborhood and headed north on Route 21, Stevie moved over on the seat and sat really close to me.

When we got near the farm, I drove along this long, bumpy dirt road through endless rows and rows of corn, straight to a place where there's a stream and a huge oak tree that has to be a hundred and fifty years old.

Stevie had brought a whole bunch of sandwiches, plus some hard-boiled eggs, hunks of cheese, potato chips, carrot sticks, and lots of those little round tomatoes the size of Ping-Pong balls, plus brownies, peaches, and grapes.

"Looks like enough food to survive on for a whole month in the wilderness," I told her.

After we ate, we took all the food that was left—there was lots—and the plates and stuff off the blanket, and then we lay down and held each other. The moment I took Stevie in my arms, she started crying.

"When my father died," she said, "it felt just like he left forever. But he never really even got to say goodbye."

I told Stevie this was different, because we weren't even

really saying "goodbye," and we had lots and lots more time to spend together. That's when we decided to call what we were saying, "So long until the next time."

"I know," she said. "I know it's not forever the way death is. It's just that sometimes that awful feeling comes back, and then I have to sort it out and realize it's not at all the same thing that's happening now."

"I want you to remember that when I'm away, Stevie," I told her.

"I will, Jeb, I'll make sure to remember," she said.

I held her closer then and kissed her until the melting feeling made us feel like we were practically one person. I wanted more than ever to make love to Stevie—really make love to her and not just the other things we've been doing instead—but I knew it wasn't the right time, just before leaving, and that it would make it harder for both of us to have me go away afterward.

I was sure Stevie felt the same.

"We're lucky, you know, because we've got time, so much time." I said. "Your father's time ran out on him, and Noel's time ran out on him. But that doesn't mean our time will run out on us."

"That's true, Jeb," Stevie said, and then we held and kissed, and then we were quiet together for a real long time, just lying on our backs on the picnic blanket watching the cloud formations float across the sky.

While we were lying there, I told Stevie how sometimes lately I have a new kind of feeling, a wonderful really full feeling about how good it is just to be alive.

"In a way," I said, "sometimes it's like I feel a double life: my own, and then another one that came to me for

Noel. It's kind of hard to explain what I mean."

"Kind of like because Noel died, because he can't live anymore, maybe you owe it to him to live a little harder?" Stevie asked, and I told her that was it exactly.

Later, when we had the car loaded up and were all set to go, I told Stevie there was one more thing I wanted to do. We picked the biggest bunch of wild flowers you've ever seen, and on our way back through Wakefield we stopped at the church where Noel is buried and left the flowers on his grave. We tried to weave them together in some nice neat arrangement like a wreath, but the flowers were too wild and tangly, with stems of different lengths and leaves and thistles stuck all through them. Finally we left them there like that, all heaped and tangled, more like a messed-up haystack than a wreath.

I can still see them now—some that were purple and bristly and some others that were soft and smooth and yellow.

ABOUT THE AUTHOR

Elizabeth Harlan is the author of *FOOTFALLS*, which *Publishers Weekly* called "a stunner." She was born in New York City and has received degrees from Barnard College and Yale Graduate School.

She lives in Cranbury, New Jersey, with her husband and two children, Joshua and Noah.